SMURFS MO

SMURFS MONSTERS

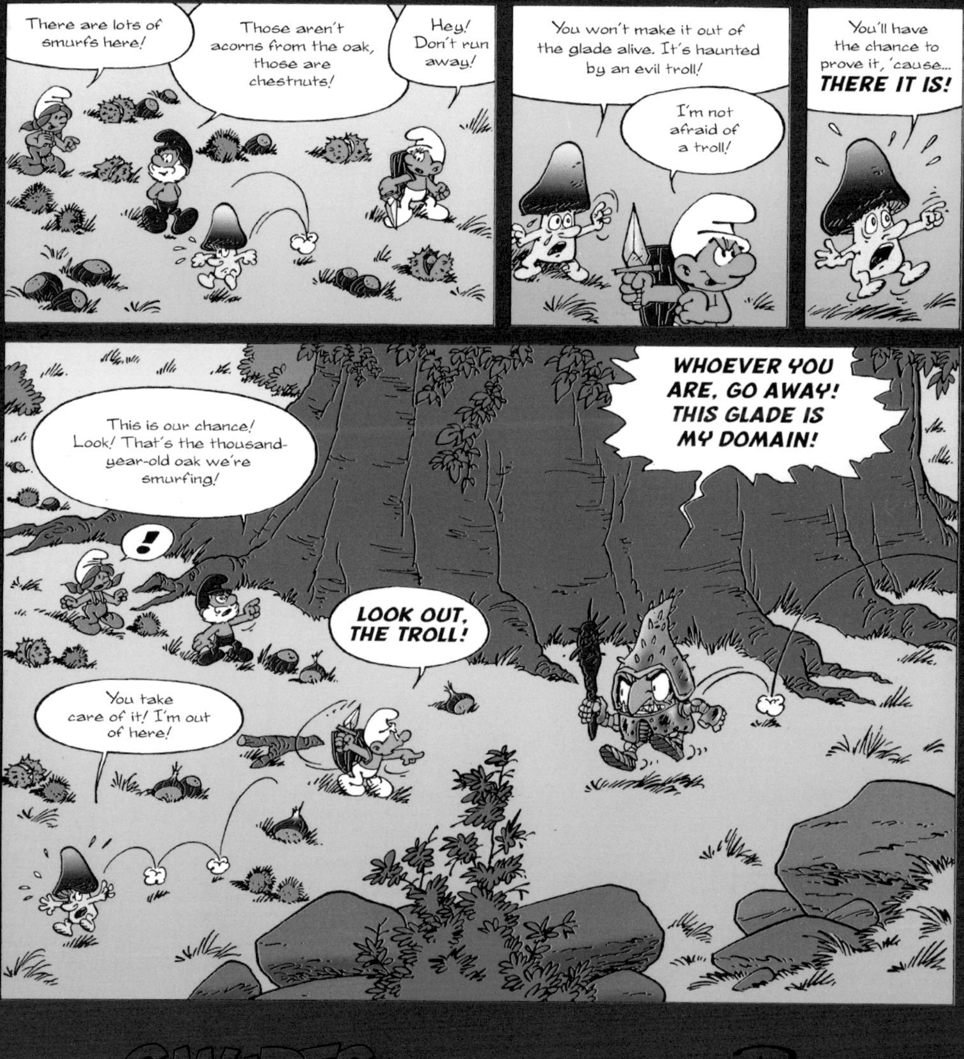
There are lots of smurfs here!
Those aren't acorns from the oak, those are chestnuts!
Hey! Don't run away!
You won't make it out of the glade alive. It's haunted by an evil troll!
I'm not afraid of a troll!
You'll have the chance to prove it, 'cause... **THERE IT IS!**
This is our chance! Look! That's the thousand-year-old oak we're smurfing!
!
WHOEVER YOU ARE, GO AWAY! THIS GLADE IS MY DOMAIN!
LOOK OUT, THE TROLL!
You take care of it! I'm out of here!

A SMURFS GRAPHIC NOVEL BY Peyo CREATIONS

PAPERCUTZ™
NEW YORK

SMURFS GRAPHIC NOVELS AVAILABLE FROM PAPERCUTZ ™

1. **THE PURPLE SMURFS**
2. **THE SMURFS AND THE MAGIC FLUTE**
3. **THE SMURF KING**
4. **THE SMURFETTE**
5. **THE SMURFS AND THE EGG**
6. **THE SMURFS AND THE HOWLIBIRD**
7. **THE ASTROSMURF**
8. **THE SMURF APPRENTICE**
9. **GARGAMEL AND THE SMURFS**
10. **THE RETURN OF THE SMURFETTE**
11. **THE SMURF OLYMPICS**
12. **SMURF VS. SMURF**
13. **SMURF SOUP**
14. **THE BABY SMURF**
15. **THE SMURFLINGS**
16. **THE AEROSMURF**
17. **THE STRANGE AWAKENING OF LAZY SMURF**
18. **THE FINANCE SMURF**
19. **THE JEWEL SMURFER**

- **THE SMURFS CHRISTMAS**
- **FOREVER SMURFETTE**
- **SMURFS MONSTERS**

THE SMURFS graphic novels are available in paperback for $5.99 each and in hardcover for $10.99 each at booksellers everywhere. You can also order online at papercutz.com. Or call 1-800-886-1223, Monday through Friday, 9 – 5 EST. MC, Visa, and AmEx accepted. To order by mail, please add $4.00 for postage and handling for first book ordered, $1.00 for each additional book and make check payable to NBM Publishing. Send to: Papercutz, 160 Broadway, Suite 700, East Wing, New York, NY 10038.

THE SMURFS graphic novels are also available digitally wherever e-books are sold.

PAPERCUTZ.COM

SMURFS MONSTERS

© Peyo - 2015 - Licensed through Lafig Belgium - www.smurf.com

English translation copyright © 2015 by Papercutz.
All rights reserved.

"Motro, the Forest Monster"
BY PEYO

"The Golden Acorns"
BY PEYO

"The Wild Carrots"
BY PEYO

"The Ice Castle"
BY PEYO

"Bigmouth and the Lizards"
BY PEYO

Joe Johnson, SMURFLATIONS
Adam Grano, SMURFIC DESIGN
Janice Chiang, LETTERING SMURFETTE
Matt. Murray, SMURF CONSULTANT
Jeff Whitman, SMURF COORDINATOR
Dani Breckenridge, SMURF INTERN
Bethany Bryan, ASSOCIATE SMURFETTE
Jim Salicrup, SMURF-IN-CHIEF

PAPERBACK EDITION ISBN: 978-1-62991-275-2
HARDCOVER EDITION ISBN: 978-1-62991-276-9

PRINTED IN CHINA SEPTEMBER 2015 BY WKT CO. LTD.
3/F PHASE 1 LEADER INDUSTRIAL CENTRE
188 TEXACO ROAD, TSEUN WAN, N.T., HONG KONG

Papercutz books may be purchased for business or promotional use. For information on bulk purchases please contact Macmillan Corporate and Premium Sales Department at (800) 221-7945 x5442.

DISTRIBUTED BY MACMILLAN
FIRST PAPERCUTZ PRINTING

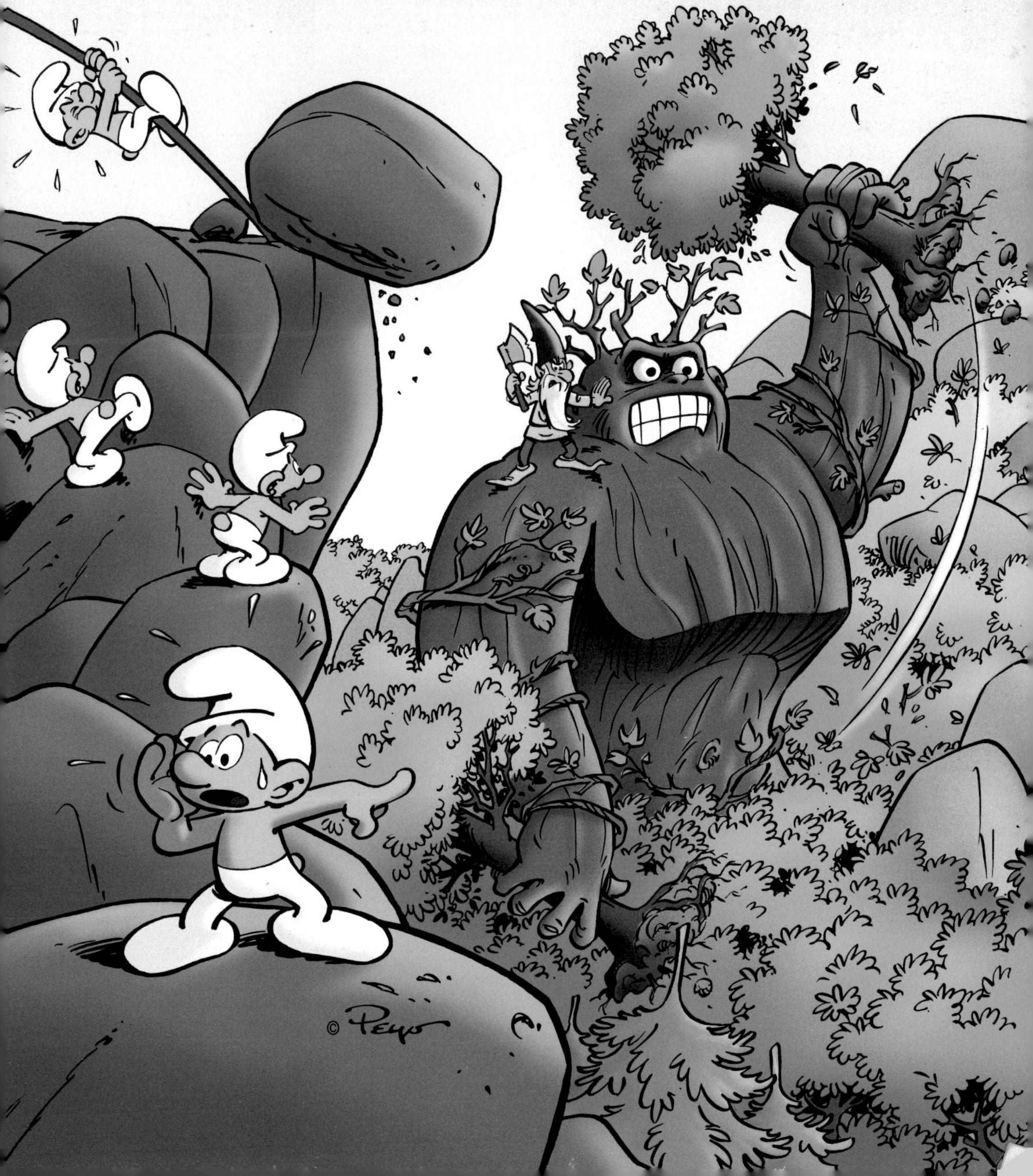
© Peyo

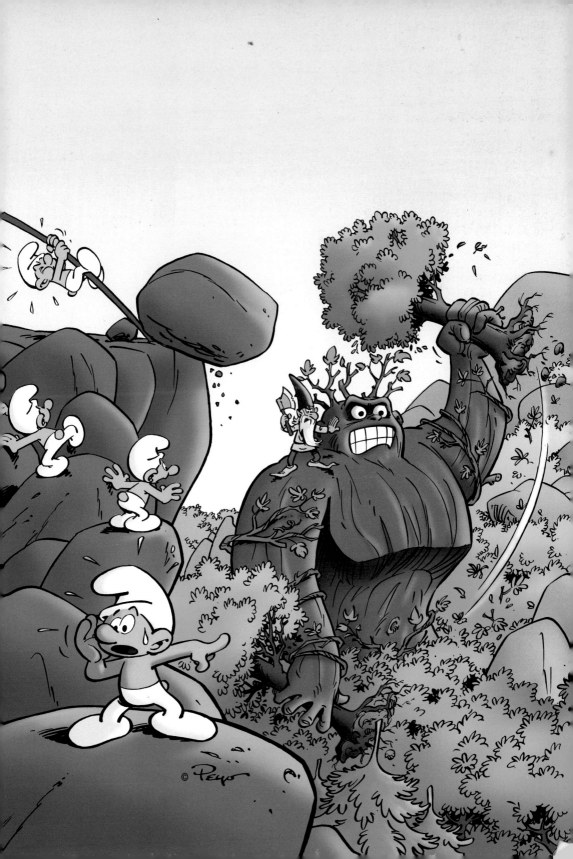

MOTRO, THE FOREST MONSTER

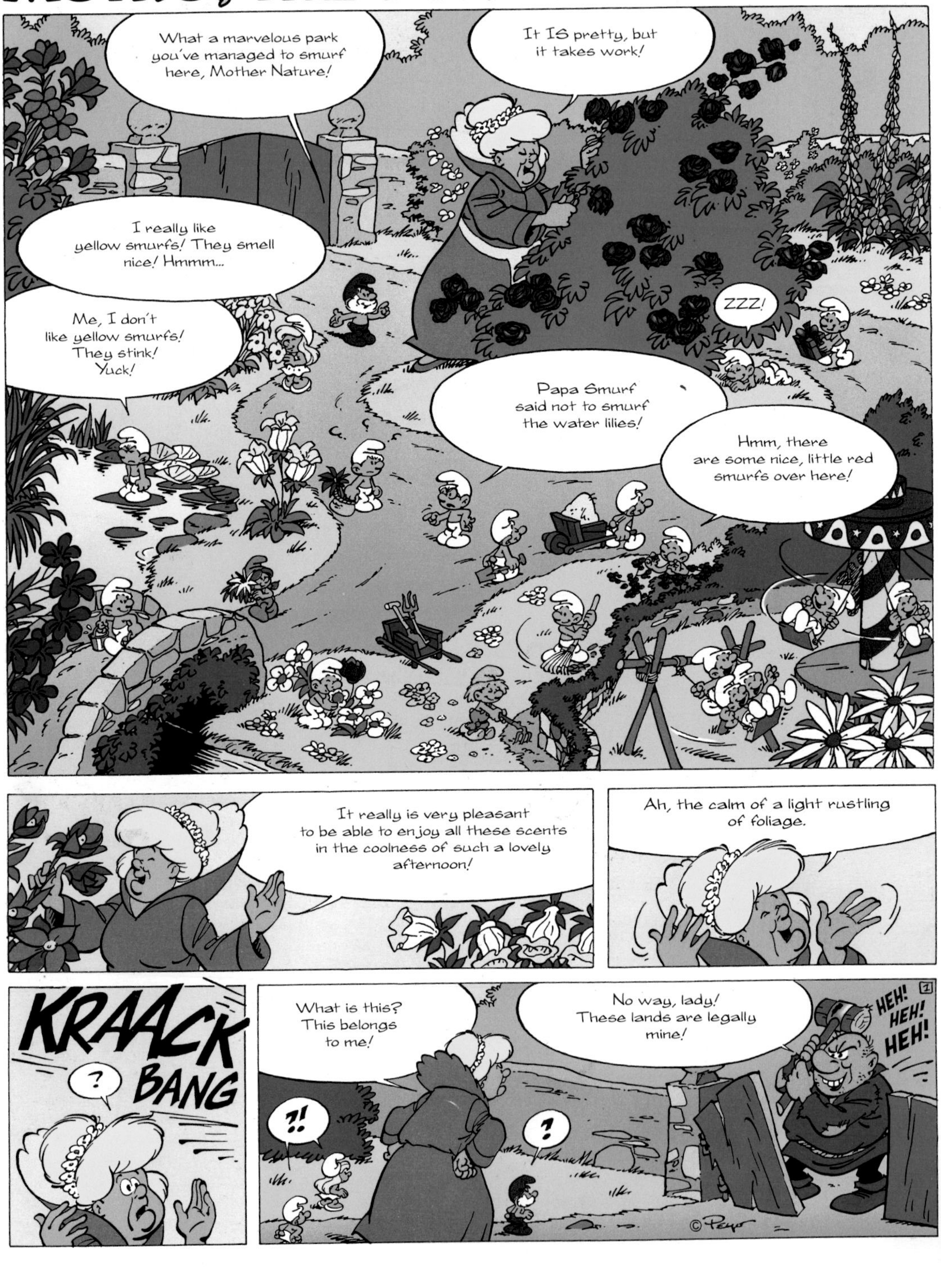
What a marvelous park you've managed to smurf here, Mother Nature!
It IS pretty, but it takes work!
I really like yellow smurfs! They smell nice! Hmmm...
Me, I don't like yellow smurfs! They stink! Yuck!
ZZZ!
Papa Smurf said not to smurf the water lilies!
Hmm, there are some nice, little red smurfs over here!
It really is very pleasant to be able to enjoy all these scents in the coolness of such a lovely afternoon!
Ah, the calm of a light rustling of foliage.
KRAACK
BANG
?
What is this? This belongs to me!
No way, lady! These lands are legally mine!
HEH! HEH! HEH!
?!
?
1
© Peyo

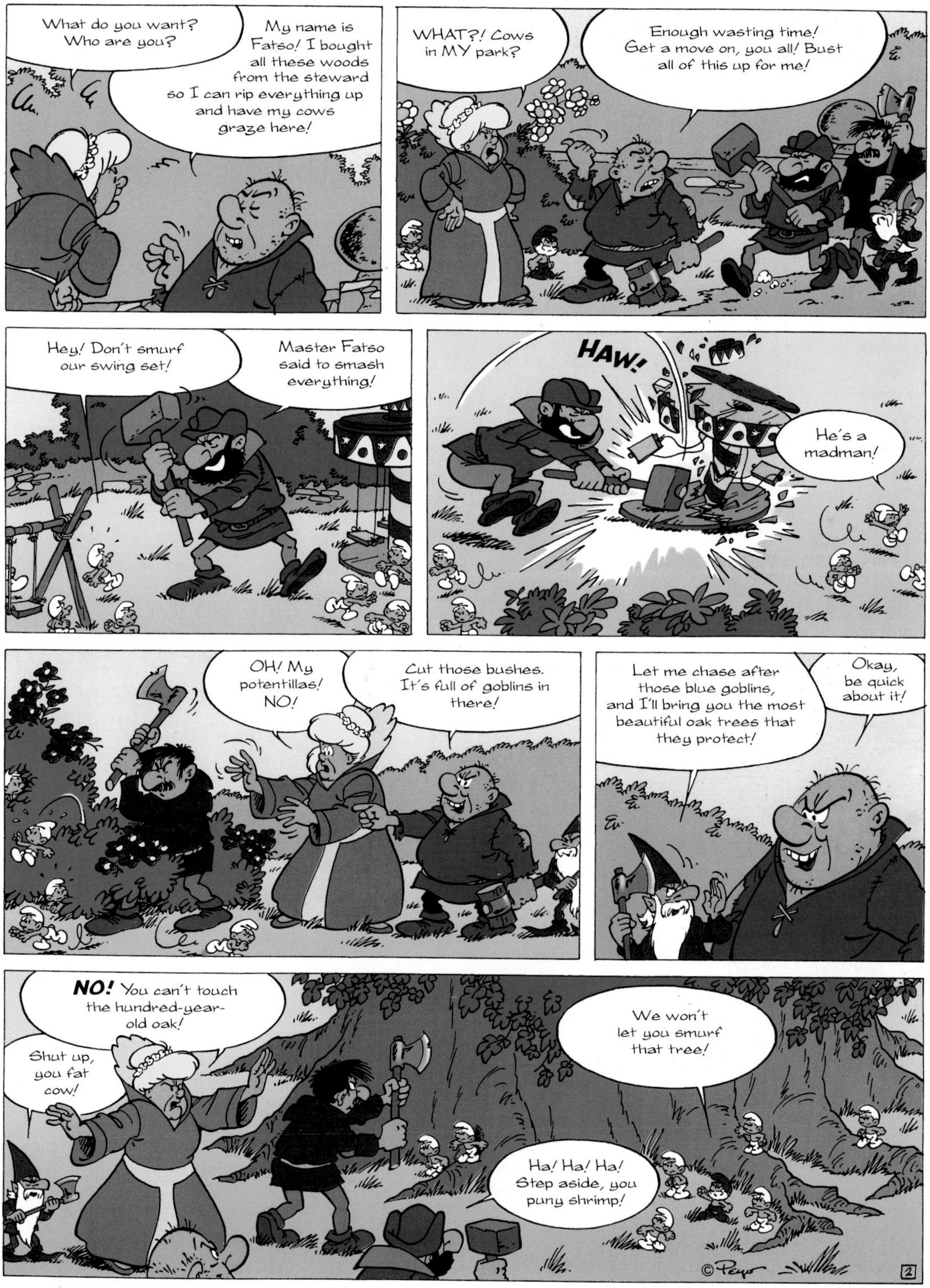
What do you want? Who are you?
My name is Fatso! I bought all these woods from the steward so I can rip everything up and have my cows graze here!
WHAT?! Cows in MY park?
Enough wasting time! Get a move on, you all! Bust all of this up for me!
Hey! Don't smurf our swing set!
Master Fatso said to smash everything!
HAW!
He's a madman!
OH! My potentillas! NO!
Cut those bushes. It's full of goblins in there!
Let me chase after those blue goblins, and I'll bring you the most beautiful oak trees that they protect!
Okay, be quick about it!
NO! You can't touch the hundred-year-old oak!
Shut up, you fat cow!
We won't let you smurf that tree!
Ha! Ha! Ha! Step aside, you puny shrimp!
© Peyo
2

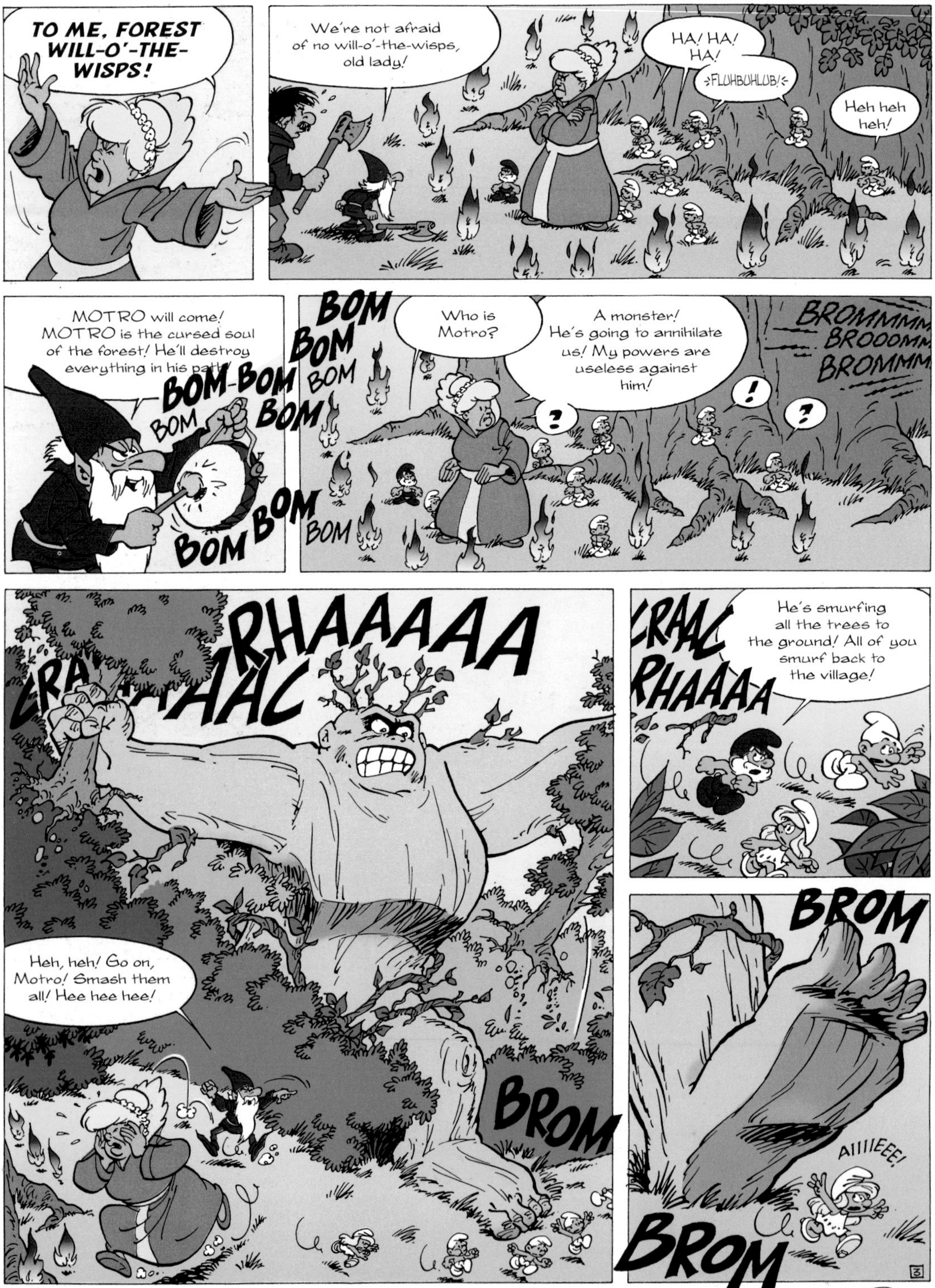
TO ME, FOREST WILL-O'-THE-WISPS!
We're not afraid of no will-o'-the-wisps, old lady!
HA! HA! HA!
FLUHBUHLUB!
Heh heh heh!
MOTRO will come! MOTRO is the cursed soul of the forest! He'll destroy everything in his path!
BOM-BOM BOM BOM BOM BOM BOM BOM
BOM BOM BOM
Who is Motro?
A monster! He's going to annihilate us! My powers are useless against him!
?
!
?
BROMMMM BROOOMM BROMMMM
RHAAAAAA
HAAC
CRAAC RHAAAA
He's smurfing all the trees to the ground! All of you smurf back to the village!
Heh, heh! Go on, Motro! Smash them all! Hee hee hee!
BROM
BROM
AIIIIEEE!
BROM
3

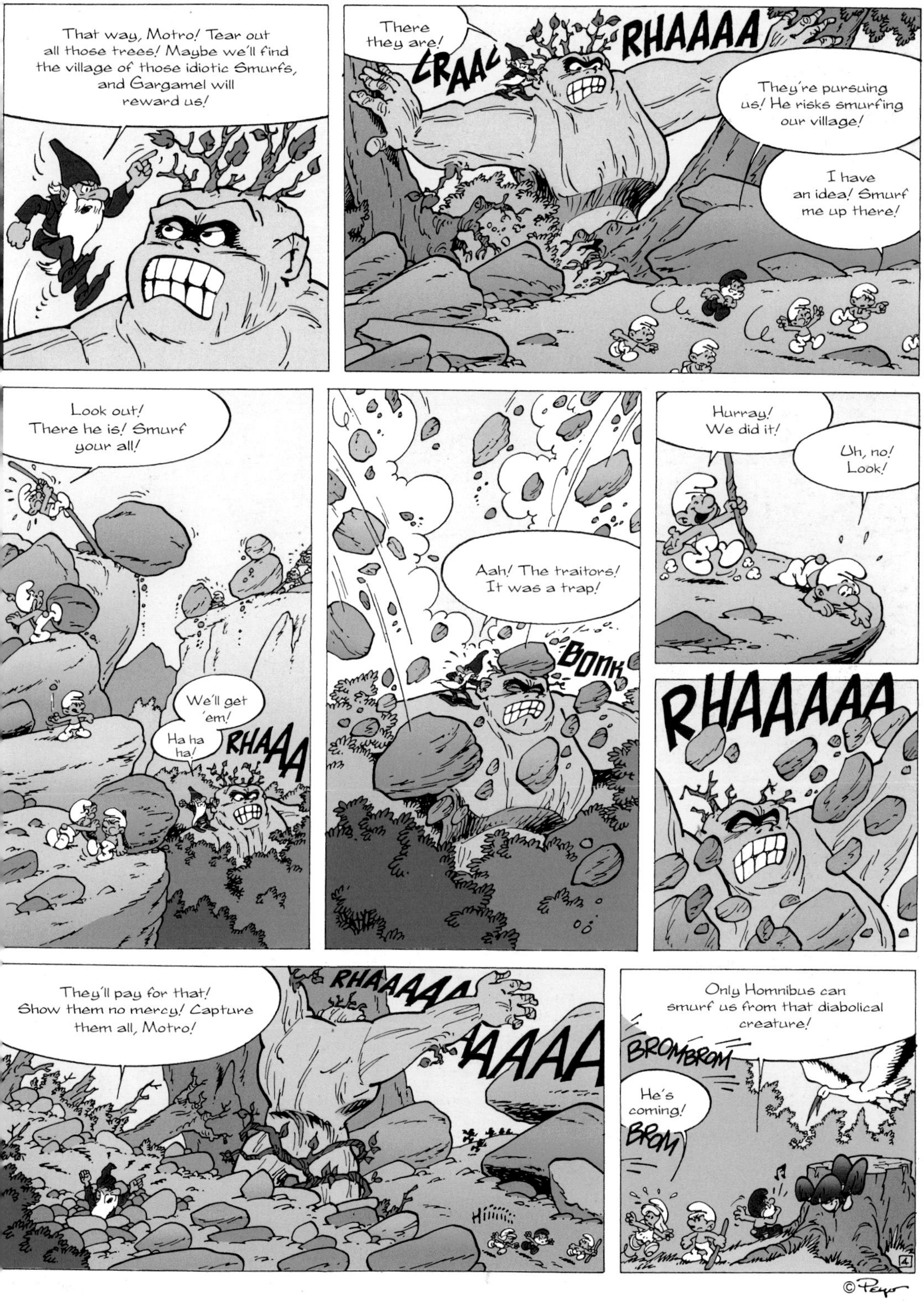
That way, Motro! Tear out all those trees! Maybe we'll find the village of those idiotic Smurfs, and Gargamel will reward us!
There they are!
CRAAC
RHAAAA
They're pursuing us! He risks smurfing our village!
I have an idea! Smurf me up there!
Look out! There he is! Smurf your all!
We'll get 'em!
Ha ha ha!
RHAAAA
Aah! The traitors! It was a trap!
BONK
Hurray! We did it!
Uh, no! Look!
RHAAAAA
They'll pay for that! Show them no mercy! Capture them all, Motro!
RHAAAAAAAAAAA
Hiiiii
Only Homnibus can smurf us from that diabolical creature!
BROMBROM
He's coming!
BROM
4
© Peyo

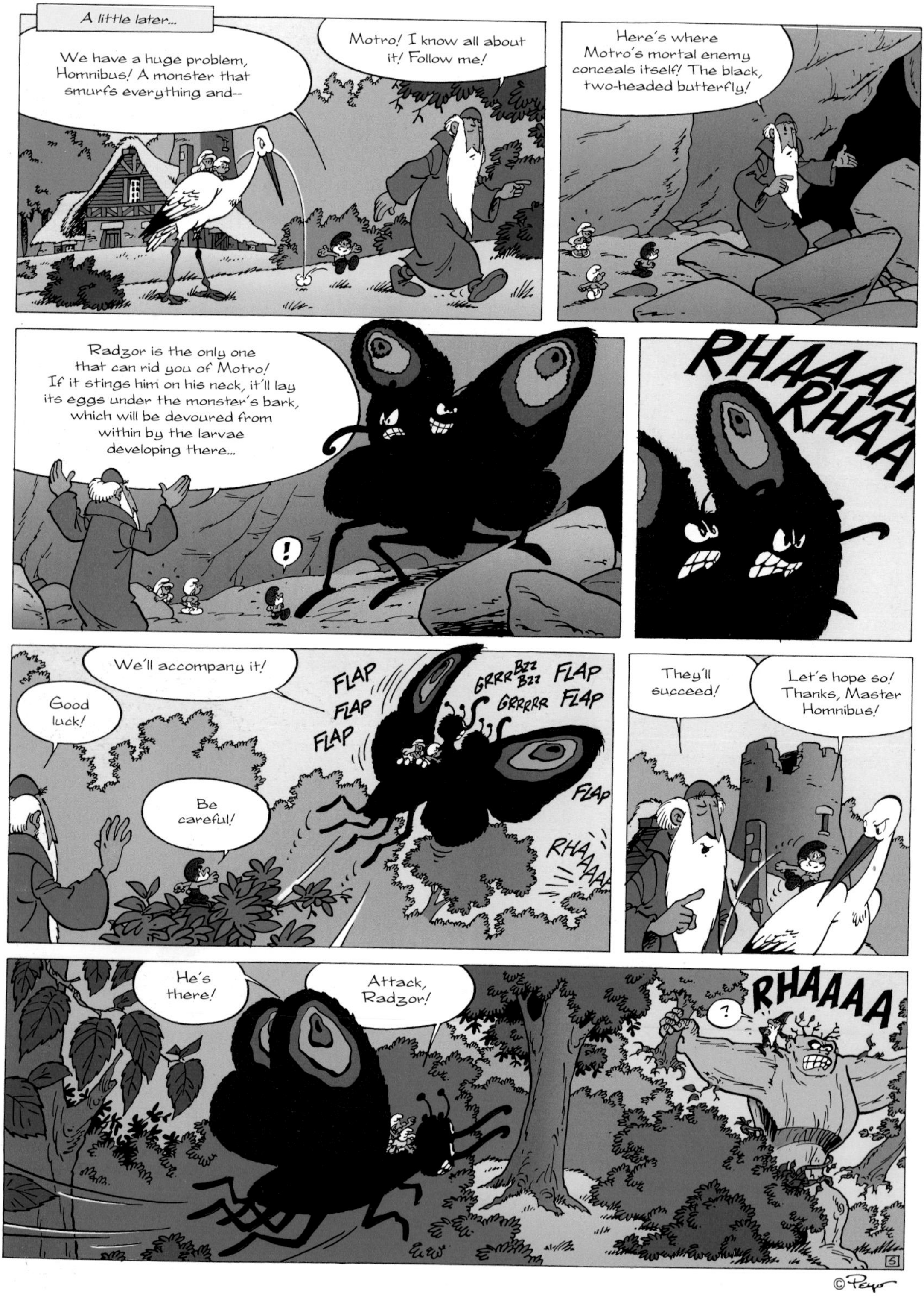
A little later...
We have a huge problem, Homnibus! A monster that smurfs everything and--
Motro! I know all about it! Follow me!
Here's where Motro's mortal enemy conceals itself! The black, two-headed butterfly!
Radzor is the only one that can rid you of Motro! If it stings him on his neck, it'll lay its eggs under the monster's bark, which will be devoured from within by the larvae developing there...
!
RHAAAA
RHAAA
We'll accompany it!
Good luck!
Be careful!
FLAP
FLAP
FLAP
GRRRR BZZ BZZ
GRRRRR
FLAP
FLAP
FLAP
RHAAAA
They'll succeed!
Let's hope so! Thanks, Master Homnibus!
He's there!
Attack, Radzor!
?
RHAAAA
5
© Peyo

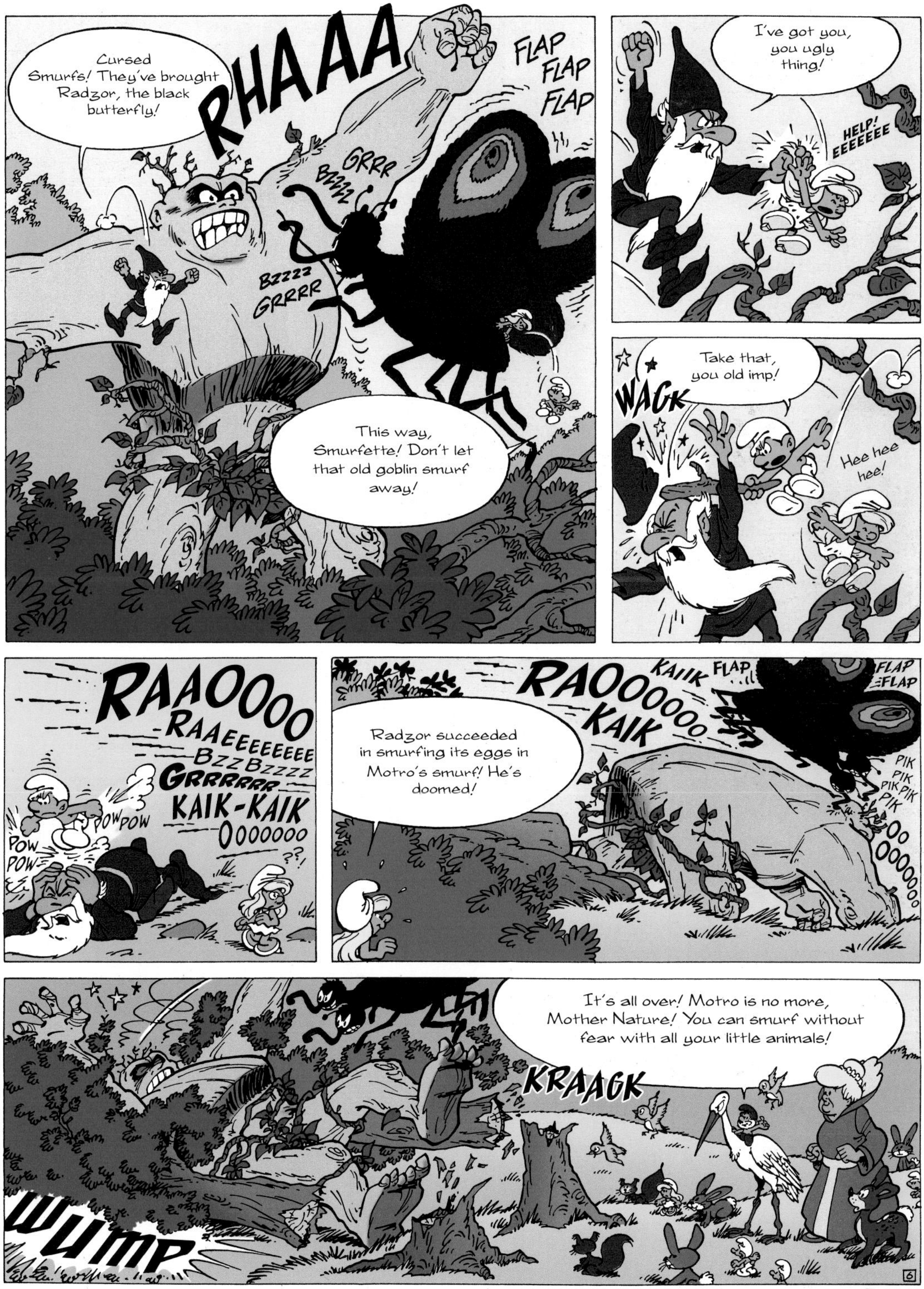
Cursed Smurfs! They've brought Radzor, the black butterfly!
RHAAA
FLAP FLAP FLAP
GRRR
BZZZZ
BZZZZ GRRRR
This way, Smurfette! Don't let that old goblin smurf away!
I've got you, you ugly thing!
HELP! EEEEEEE
WAGK
Take that, you old imp!
Hee hee hee!
RAAOOOO
RAAEEEEEEEE
BZZBZZZZ
GRRRRRRR
KAIK-KAIK
OOOOOOO
POW POW
POW POW
KAIK FLAP
RAOOOOOOO KAIK
FLAP FLAP
Radzor succeeded in smurfing its eggs in Motro's smurf! He's doomed!
PIK PIK PIK PIK PIK
OO OOOOOO
It's all over! Motro is no more, Mother Nature! You can smurf without fear with all your little animals!
KRAAGK
WUMP
6
© Peyo

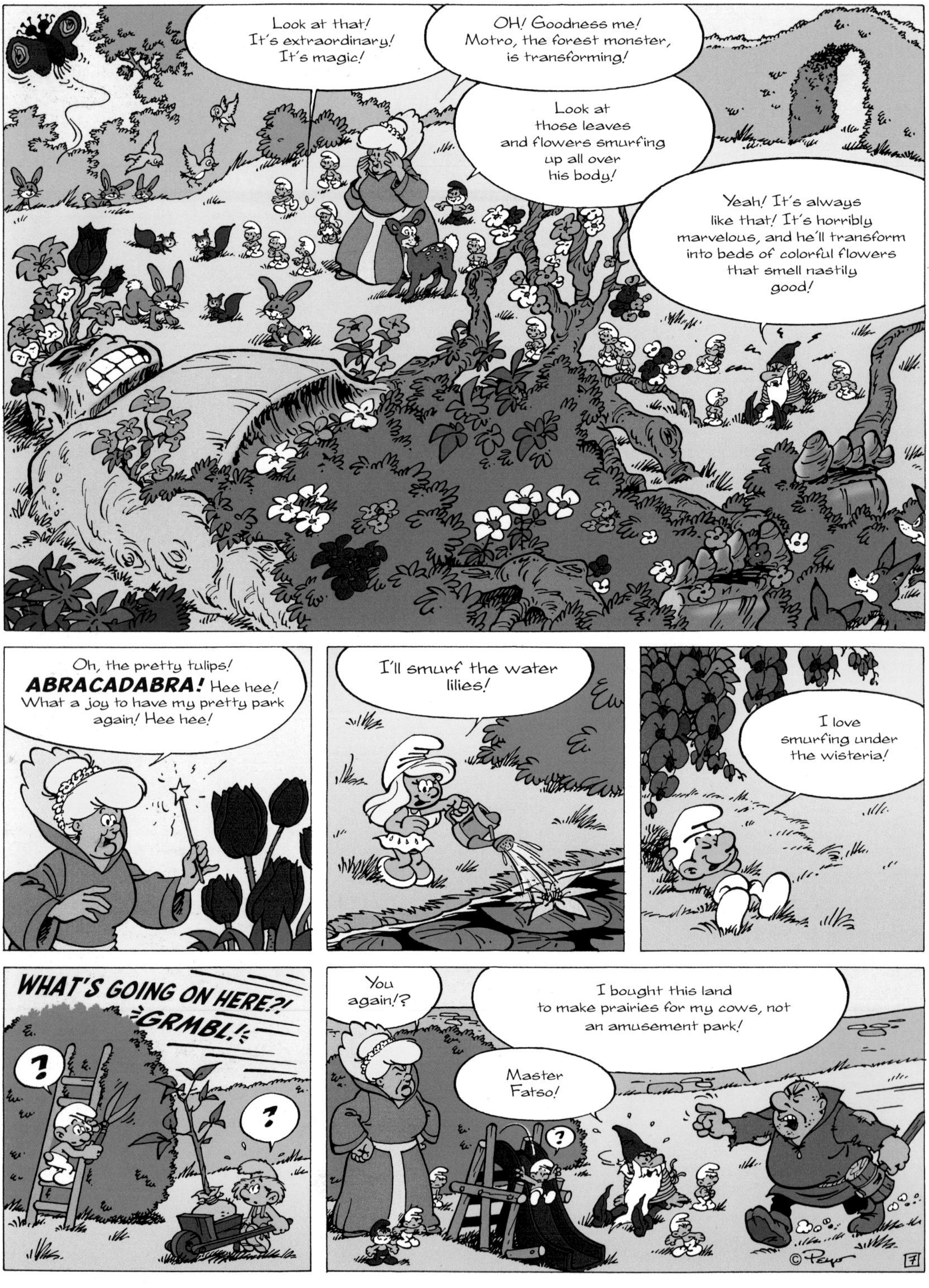
Look at that! It's extraordinary! It's magic!
OH! Goodness me! Motro, the forest monster, is transforming!
Look at those leaves and flowers smurfing up all over his body!
Yeah! It's always like that! It's horribly marvelous, and he'll transform into beds of colorful flowers that smell nastily good!
Oh, the pretty tulips! ABRACADABRA! Hee hee! What a joy to have my pretty park again! Hee hee!
I'll smurf the water lilies!
I love smurfing under the wisteria!
WHAT'S GOING ON HERE?! GRMBL!
?
?
You again!?
I bought this land to make prairies for my cows, not an amusement park!
Master Fatso!
?
© Peyo
7

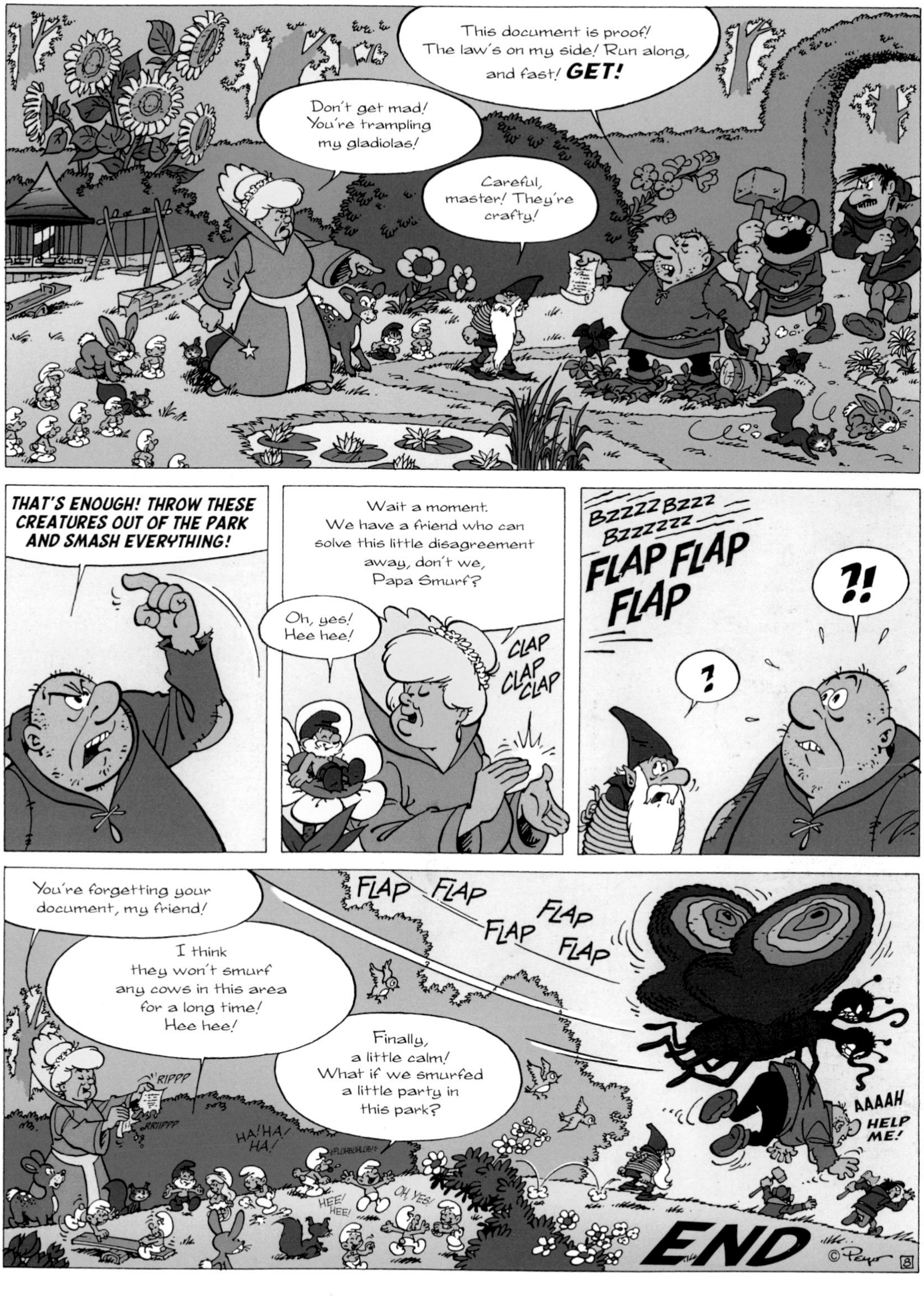
Don't get mad! You're trampling my gladiolas!
This document is proof! The law's on my side! Run along, and fast! GET!
Careful, master! They're crafty!
THAT'S ENOUGH! THROW THESE CREATURES OUT OF THE PARK AND SMASH EVERYTHING!
Wait a moment. We have a friend who can solve this little disagreement away, don't we, Papa Smurf?
Oh, yes! Hee hee!
CLAP CLAP CLAP
BZZZZ BZZZ BZZZZZZ
FLAP FLAP FLAP
?!
?
You're forgetting your document, my friend!
I think they won't smurf any cows in this area for a long time! Hee hee!
RIPPP
RRIIPPP
HA! HA! HA!
FLOHBUHLUB!
Finally, a little calm! What if we smurfed a little party in this park?
HEE! HEE!
OH, YES!
FLAP FLAP FLAP FLAP FLAP
AAAAH HELP ME!
END
© Peyo
8

THE GOLDEN ACORNS

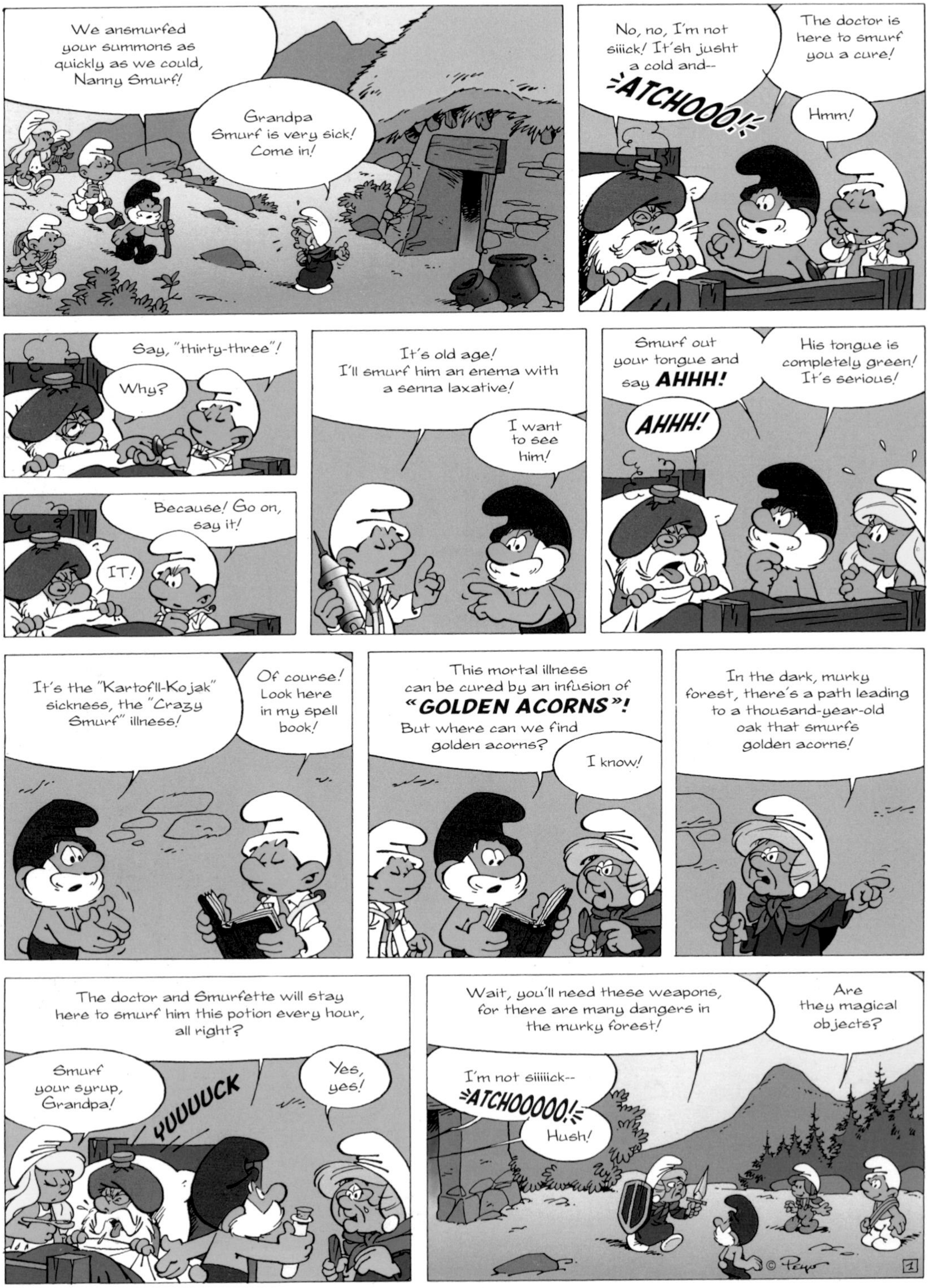

We ansmurfed your summons as quickly as we could, Nanny Smurf!
Grandpa Smurf is very sick! Come in!
No, no, I'm not siiick! It'sh jusht a cold and--
ATCHOOO!
The doctor is here to smurf you a cure!
Hmm!
Say, "thirty-three"!
Why?
Because! Go on, say it!
IT!
It's old age! I'll smurf him an enema with a senna laxative!
I want to see him!
Smurf out your tongue and say AHHH!
AHHH!
His tongue is completely green! It's serious!
It's the "Kartofll-Kojak" sickness, the "Crazy Smurf" illness!
Of course! Look here in my spell book!
This mortal illness can be cured by an infusion of "GOLDEN ACORNS"! But where can we find golden acorns?
I know!
In the dark, murky forest, there's a path leading to a thousand-year-old oak that smurfs golden acorns!
The doctor and Smurfette will stay here to smurf him this potion every hour, all right?
Smurf your syrup, Grandpa!
YUUUUCK
Yes, yes!
Wait, you'll need these weapons, for there are many dangers in the murky forest!
Are they magical objects?
I'm not siiiick--
ATCHOOOOO!
Hush!
© Peyo
1

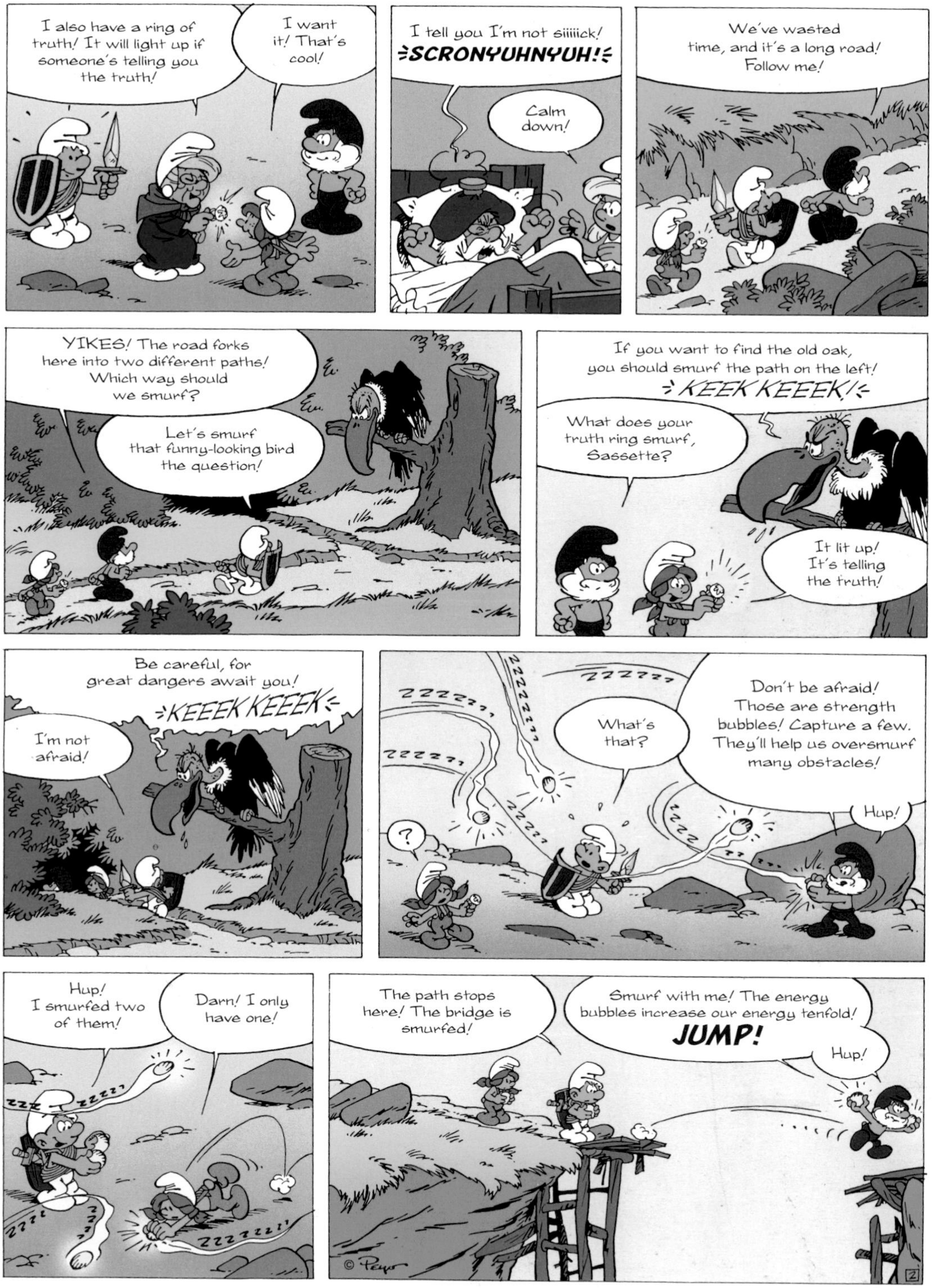
I also have a ring of truth! It will light up if someone's telling you the truth!
I want it! That's cool!
I tell you I'm not siiiiick!
SCRONYUHNYUH!
Calm down!
We've wasted time, and it's a long road! Follow me!
YIKES! The road forks here into two different paths! Which way should we smurf?
Let's smurf that funny-looking bird the question!
If you want to find the old oak, you should smurf the path on the left!
KEEK KEEEK!
What does your truth ring smurf, Sassette?
It lit up! It's telling the truth!
Be careful, for great dangers await you!
KEEEK KEEEK
I'm not afraid!
What's that?
Don't be afraid! Those are strength bubbles! Capture a few. They'll help us oversmurf many obstacles!
Hup!
Hup! I smurfed two of them!
Darn! I only have one!
The path stops here! The bridge is smurfed!
Smurf with me! The energy bubbles increase our energy tenfold! JUMP!
Hup!
© Peyo
2

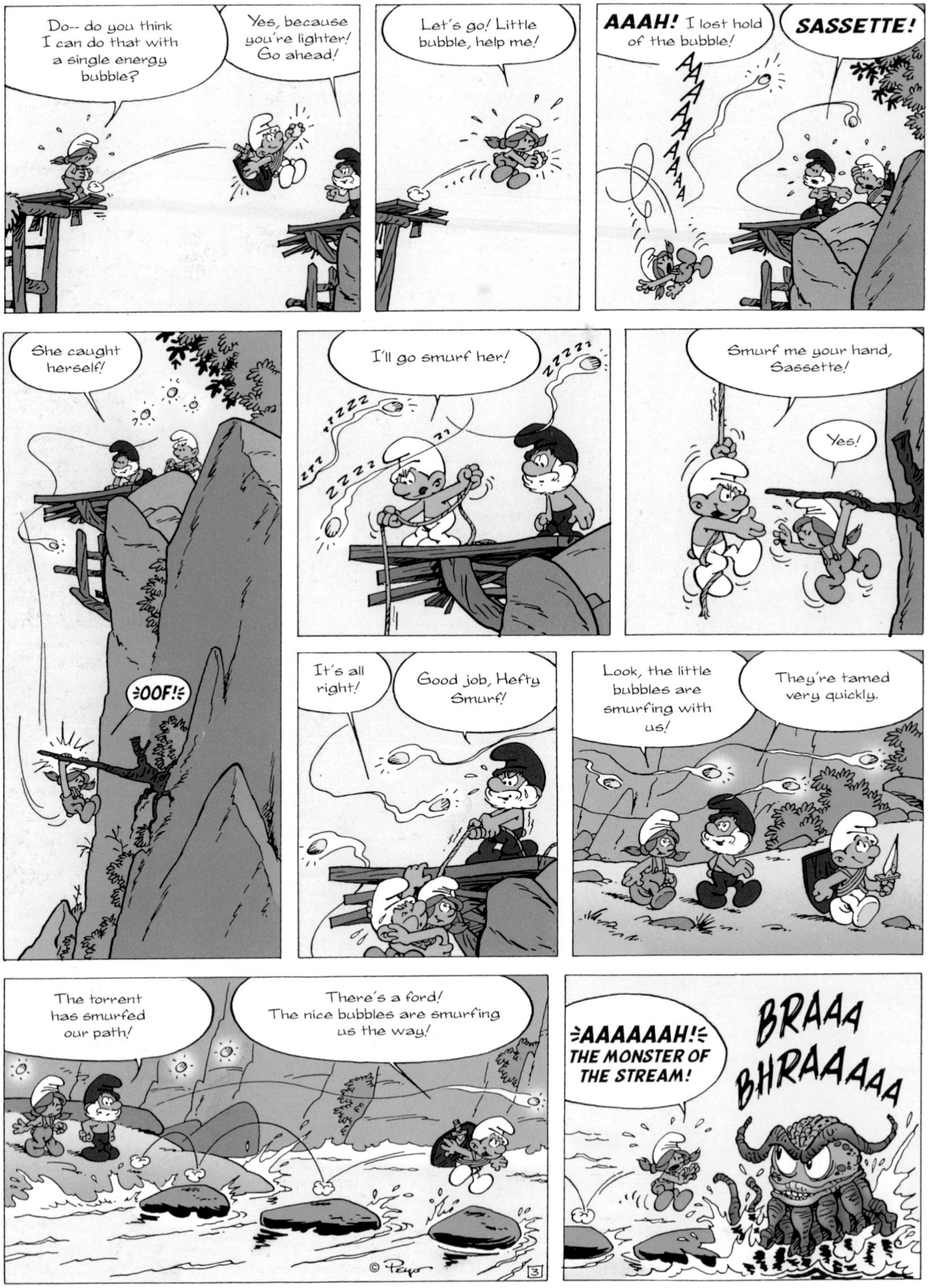
Do-- do you think I can do that with a single energy bubble?
Yes, because you're lighter! Go ahead!
Let's go! Little bubble, help me!
AAAH! I lost hold of the bubble!
AAAAAAAAA
SASSETTE!
She caught herself!
OOF!
I'll go smurf her!
Smurf me your hand, Sassette!
Yes!
It's all right!
Good job, Hefty Smurf!
Look, the little bubbles are smurfing with us!
They're tamed very quickly.
The torrent has smurfed our path!
There's a ford! The nice bubbles are smurfing us the way!
© Peyo
3
AAAAAAH! THE MONSTER OF THE STREAM!
BRAAA BHRAAAAA

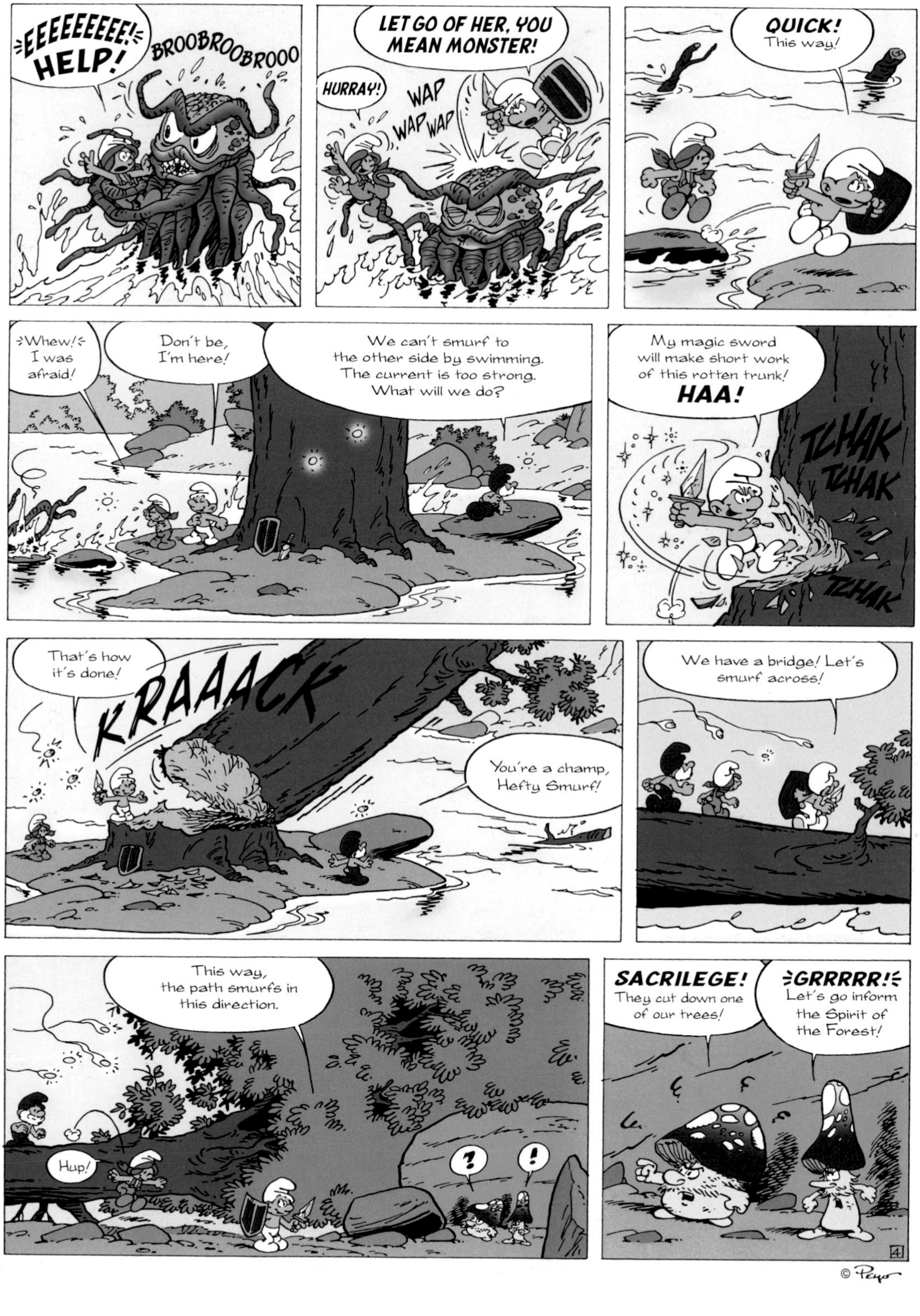
EEEEEEEEE! HELP!
BROOBROOBROOO
LET GO OF HER, YOU MEAN MONSTER!
HURRAY!
WAP WAP WAP
QUICK! This way!
Whew! I was afraid!
Don't be, I'm here!
We can't smurf to the other side by swimming. The current is too strong. What will we do?
My magic sword will make short work of this rotten trunk! HAA!
TCHAK TCHAK
TCHAK
That's how it's done!
KRAAACK
You're a champ, Hefty Smurf!
We have a bridge! Let's smurf across!
This way, the path smurfs in this direction.
Hup!
?
!
SACRILEGE! They cut down one of our trees!
GRRRRR! Let's go inform the Spirit of the Forest!
4
© Peyo

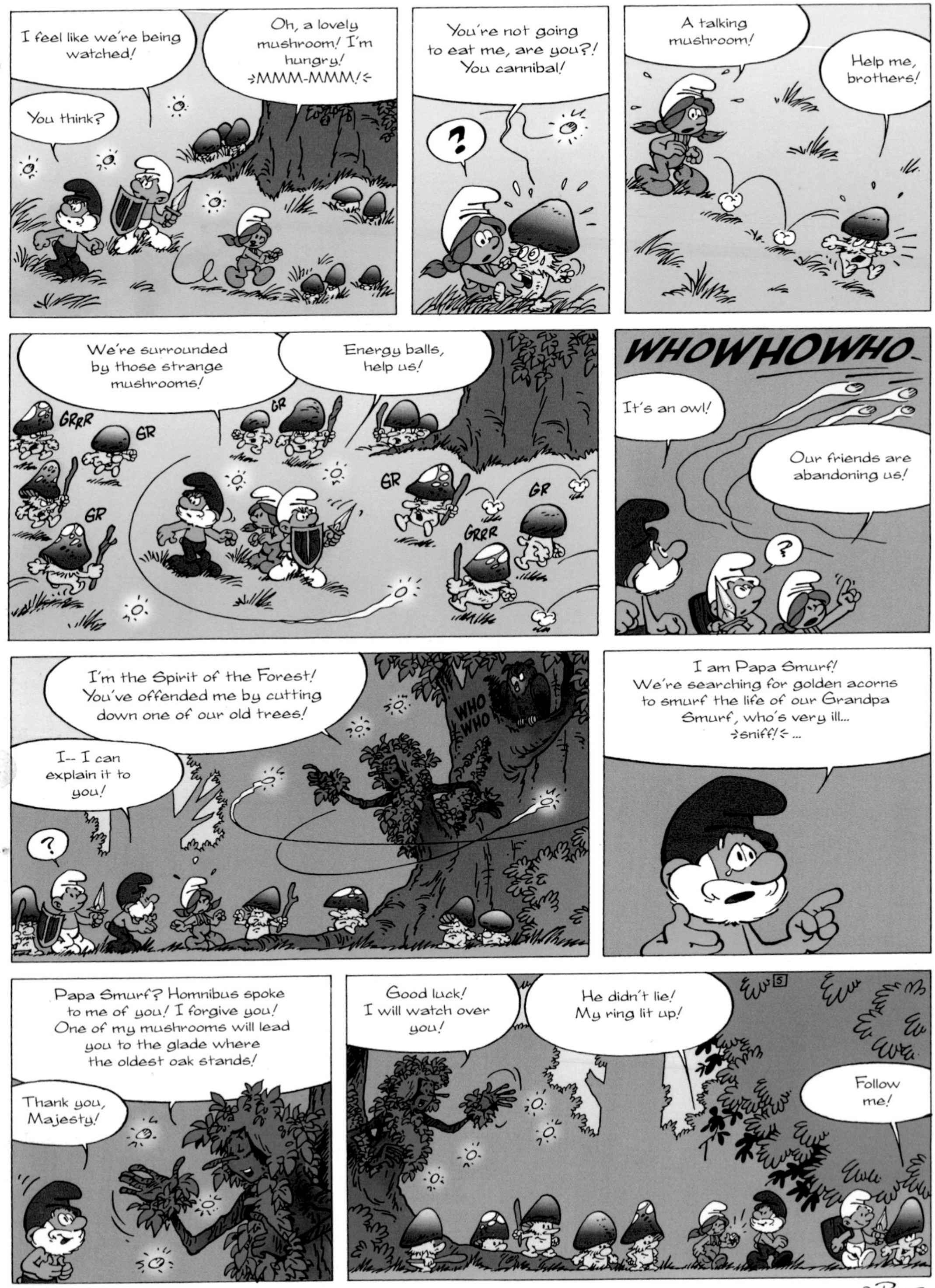
I feel like we're being watched!
Oh, a lovely mushroom! I'm hungry! >MMM-MMM!<
You think?
You're not going to eat me, are you?! You cannibal!
?
A talking mushroom!
Help me, brothers!
We're surrounded by those strange mushrooms!
Energy balls, help us!
GRRR
GR
GR
GR
GR
GR
GRRR
WHOWHOWHO
It's an owl!
Our friends are abandoning us!
?
I'm the Spirit of the Forest! You've offended me by cutting down one of our old trees!
I-- I can explain it to you!
?
WHO WHO
I am Papa Smurf! We're searching for golden acorns to smurf the life of our Grandpa Smurf, who's very ill... >sniff!< ...
Papa Smurf? Homnibus spoke to me of you! I forgive you! One of my mushrooms will lead you to the glade where the oldest oak stands!
Thank you, Majesty!
Good luck! I will watch over you!
He didn't lie! My ring lit up!
Follow me!

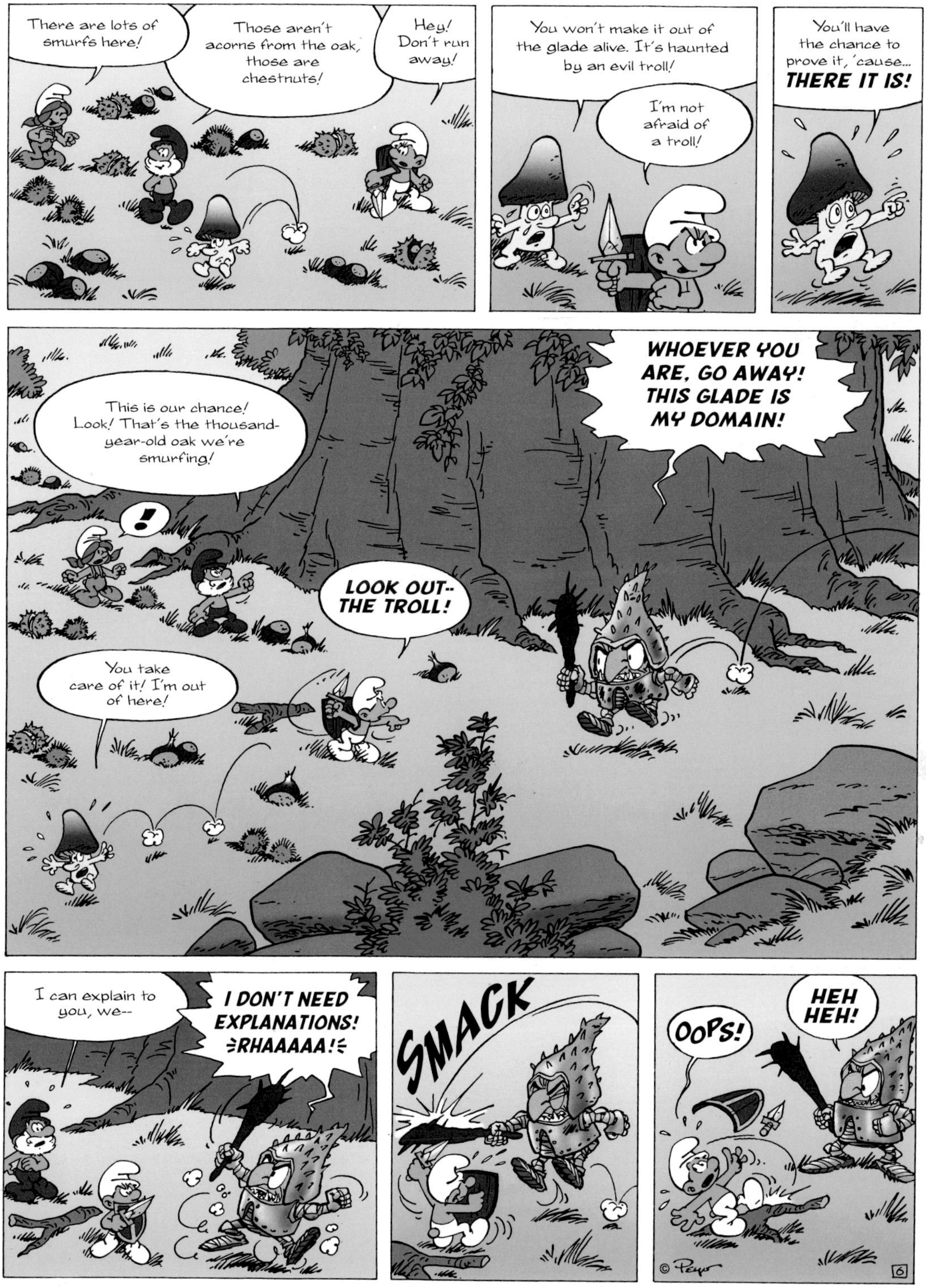
There are lots of smurfs here!
Those aren't acorns from the oak, those are chestnuts!
Hey! Don't run away!
You won't make it out of the glade alive. It's haunted by an evil troll!
I'm not afraid of a troll!
You'll have the chance to prove it, 'cause... THERE IT IS!
This is our chance! Look! That's the thousand-year-old oak we're smurfing!
WHOEVER YOU ARE, GO AWAY! THIS GLADE IS MY DOMAIN!
!
LOOK OUT-- THE TROLL!
You take care of it! I'm out of here!
I can explain to you, we--
I DON'T NEED EXPLANATIONS! RHAAAAA!
SMACK
OOPS!
HEH HEH!
© Peyo
6

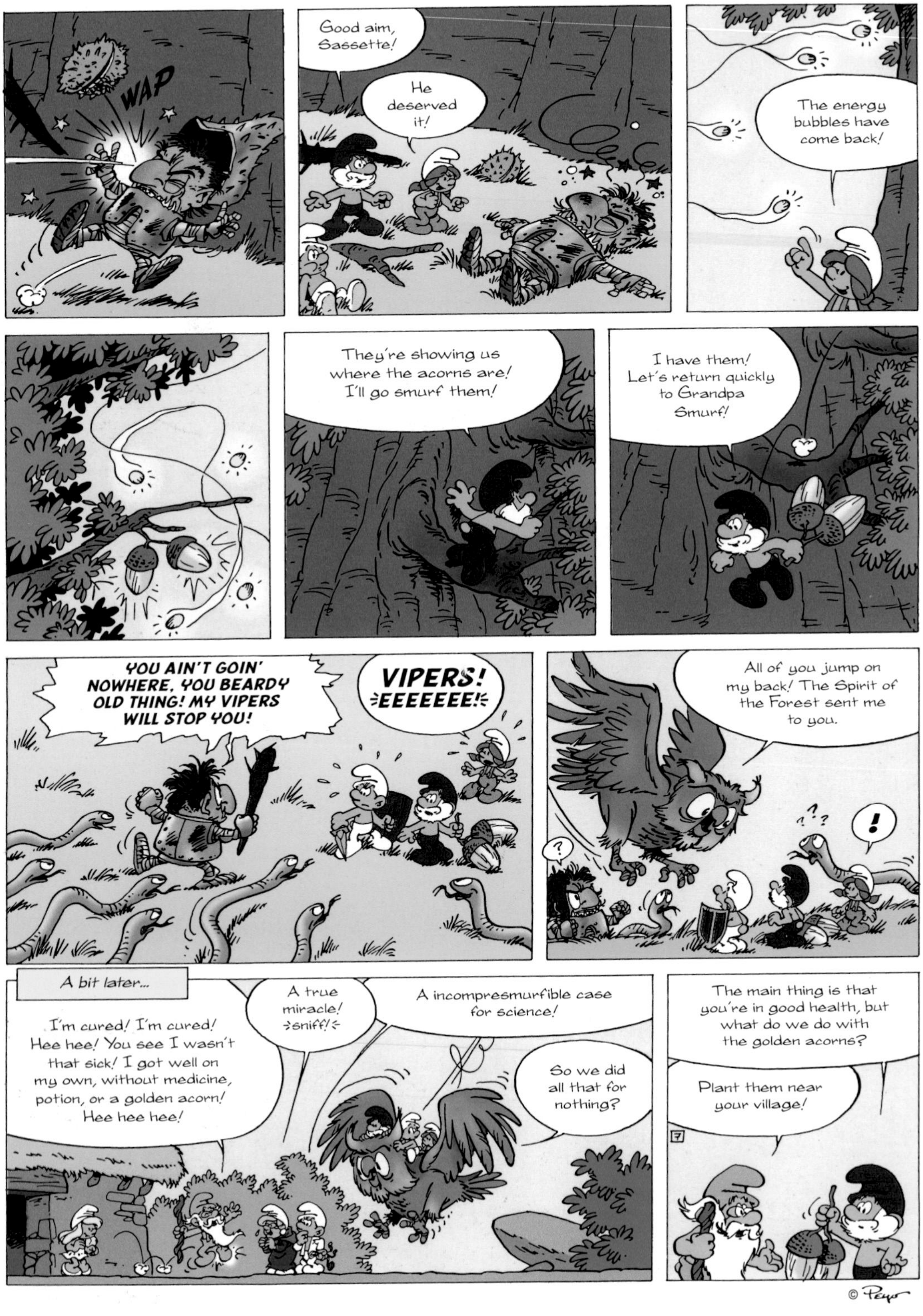
WAP
Good aim, Sassette!
He deserved it!
The energy bubbles have come back!
They're showing us where the acorns are! I'll go smurf them!
I have them! Let's return quickly to Grandpa Smurf!
YOU AIN'T GOIN' NOWHERE, YOU BEARDY OLD THING! MY VIPERS WILL STOP YOU!
VIPERS! EEEEEEE!
All of you jump on my back! The Spirit of the Forest sent me to you.
?
??
!
A bit later...
I'm cured! I'm cured! Hee hee! You see I wasn't that sick! I got well on my own, without medicine, potion, or a golden acorn! Hee hee hee!
A true miracle! sniff!
A incompresmurfible case for science!
So we did all that for nothing?
The main thing is that you're in good health, but what do we do with the golden acorns?
Plant them near your village!
7
© Peyo

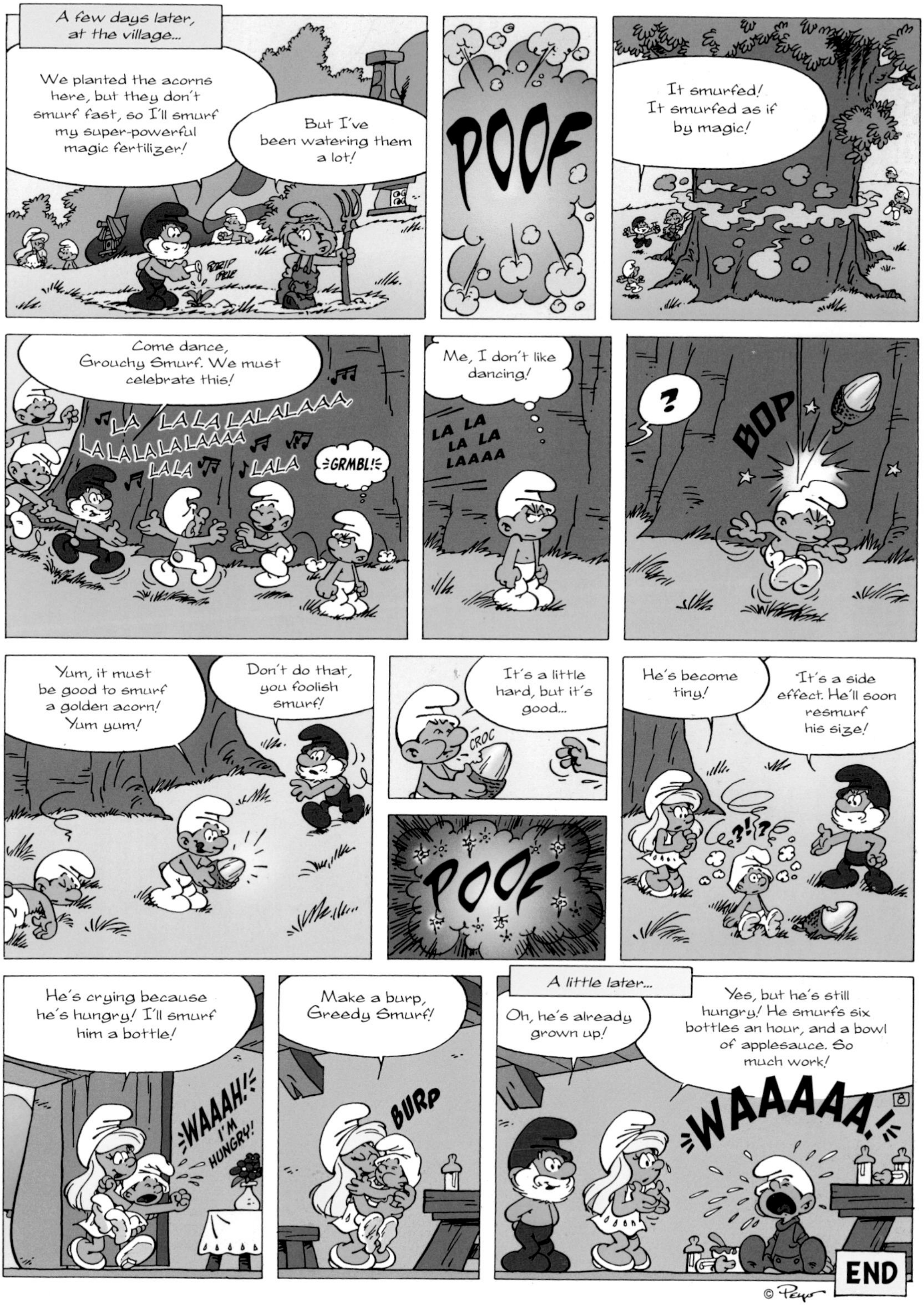
A few days later, at the village...
We planted the acorns here, but they don't smurf fast, so I'll smurf my super-powerful magic fertilizer!
But I've been watering them a lot!
POOF
It smurfed! It smurfed as if by magic!
Come dance, Grouchy Smurf. We must celebrate this!
LA LA LA LALALAAA
LALALALALAAAA
LALA
LALA
GRMBL!
Me, I don't like dancing!
LA LA LA LA LAAAA
?
BOP
Yum, it must be good to smurf a golden acorn! Yum yum!
Don't do that, you foolish smurf!
It's a little hard, but it's good...
CROC
POOF
He's become tiny!
It's a side effect. He'll soon resmurf his size!
?!?
He's crying because he's hungry! I'll smurf him a bottle!
WAAAH! I'M HUNGRY!
Make a burp, Greedy Smurf!
BURP
A little later...
Oh, he's already grown up!
Yes, but he's still hungry! He smurfs six bottles an hour, and a bowl of applesauce. So much work!
WAAAAA!
END
© Peyo

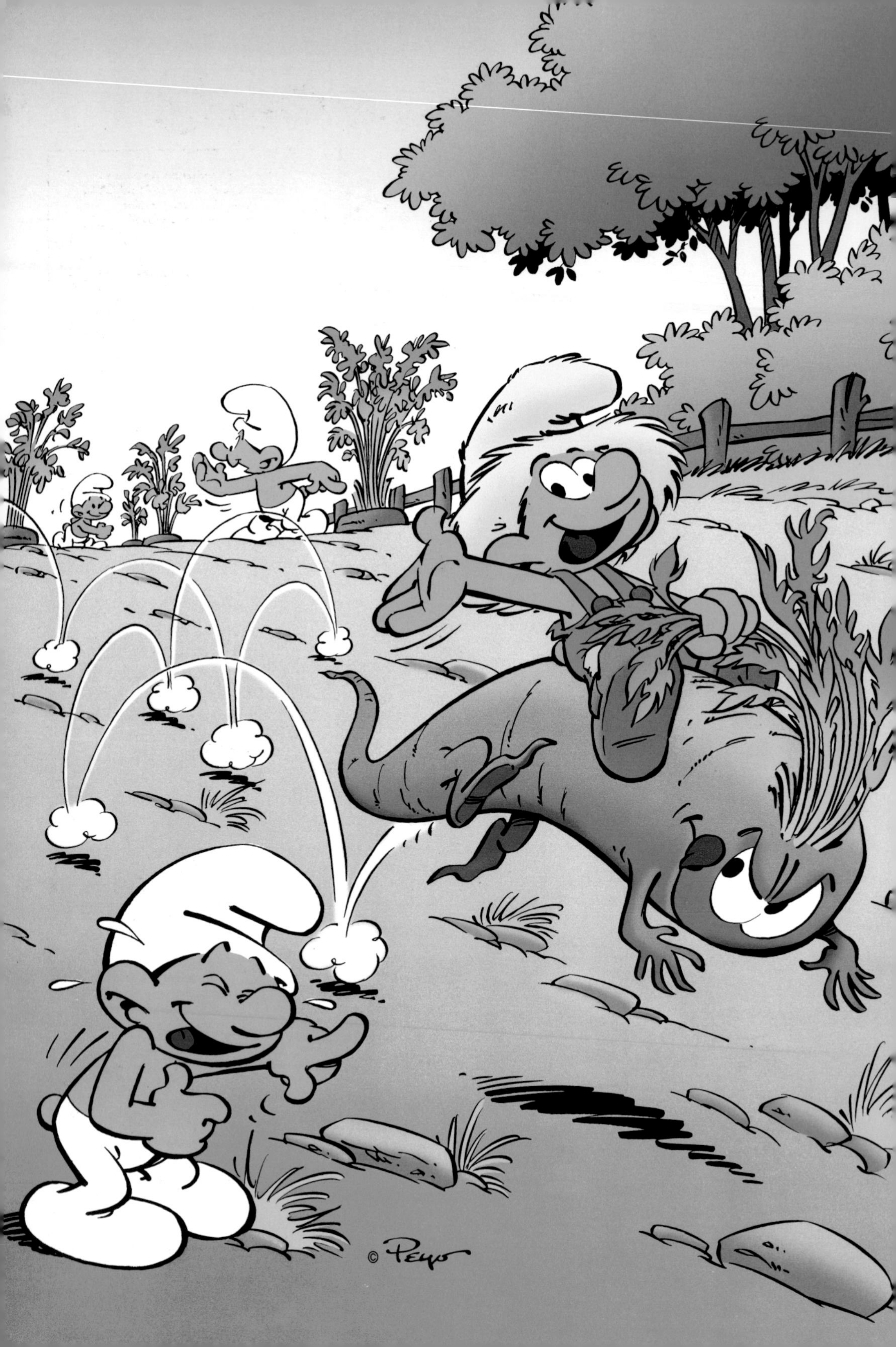
© Peyo

THE WILD CARROTS

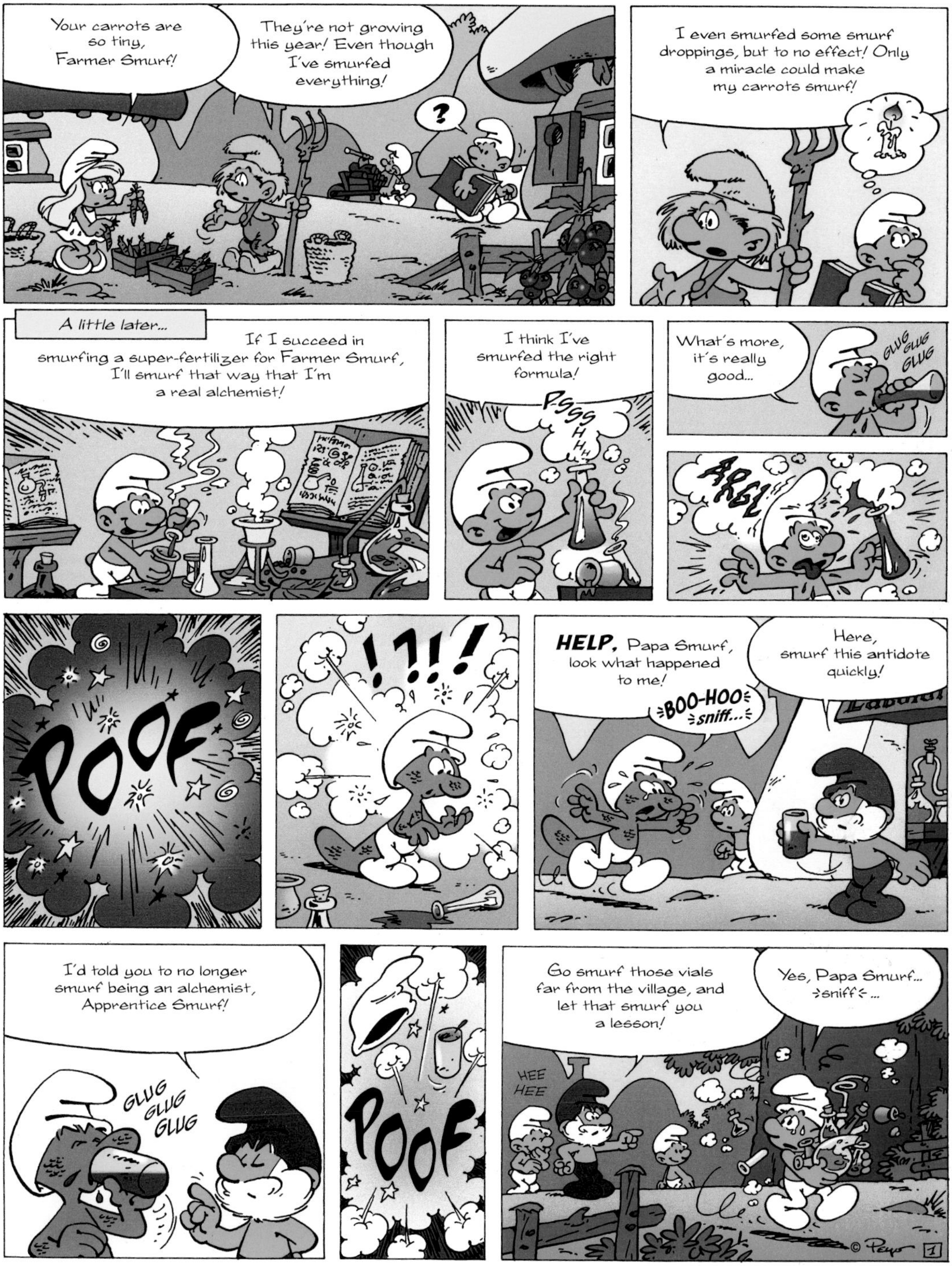
Your carrots are so tiny, Farmer Smurf!
They're not growing this year! Even though I've smurfed everything!
?
I even smurfed some smurf droppings, but to no effect! Only a miracle could make my carrots smurf!
A little later...
If I succeed in smurfing a super-fertilizer for Farmer Smurf, I'll smurf that way that I'm a real alchemist!
I think I've smurfed the right formula!
PSSSHHH
What's more, it's really good...
GLUG GLUG GLUG
ARGL
POOF
!?!!
HELP, Papa Smurf, look what happened to me!
BOO-HOO sniff...
Here, smurf this antidote quickly!
I'd told you to no longer smurf being an alchemist, Apprentice Smurf!
GLUG GLUG GLUG
POOF
Go smurf those vials far from the village, and let that smurf you a lesson!
Yes, Papa Smurf... sniff ...
HEE HEE
© Peyo
1

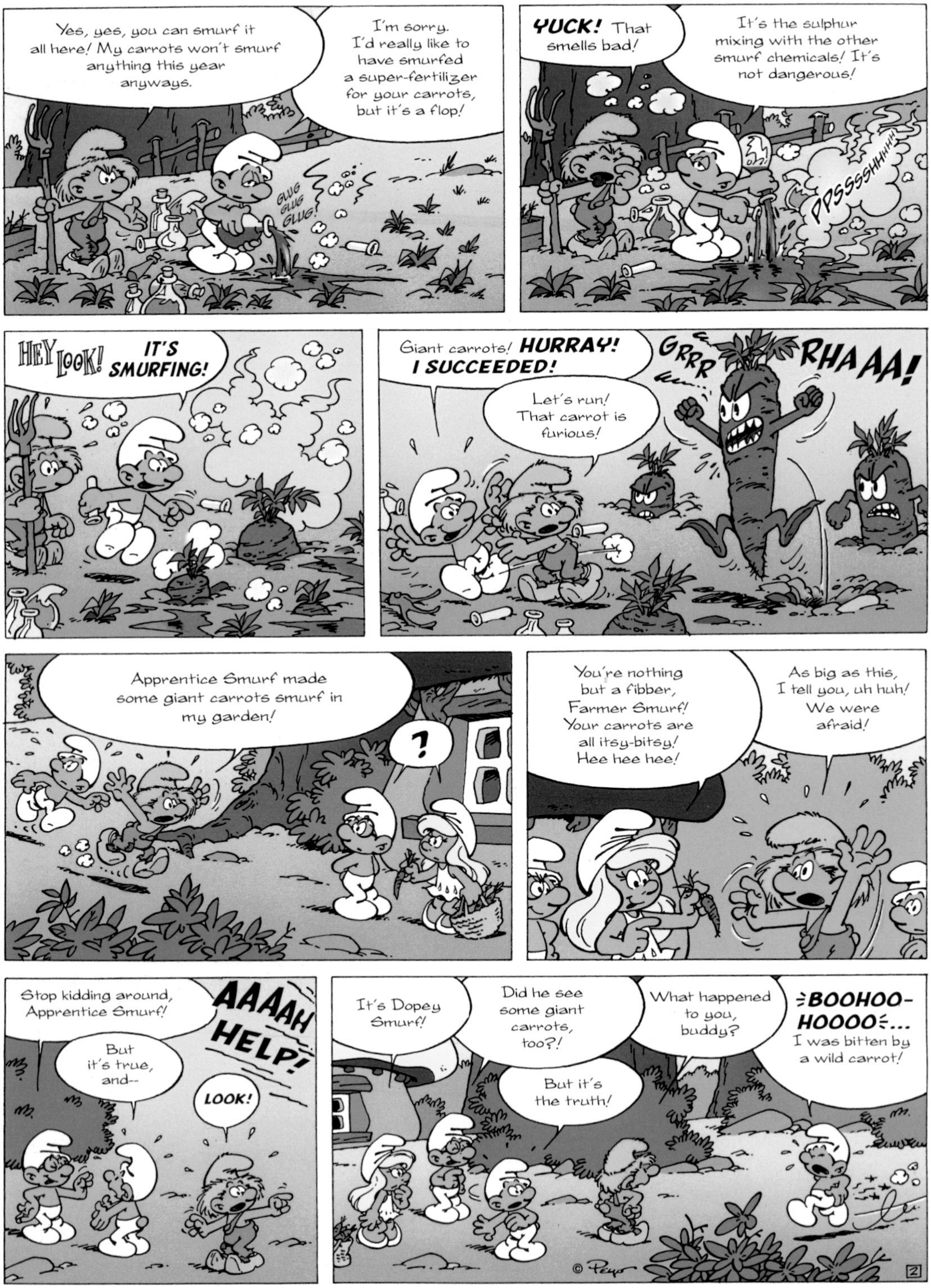
Yes, yes, you can smurf it all here! My carrots won't smurf anything this year anyways.
I'm sorry. I'd really like to have smurfed a super-fertilizer for your carrots, but it's a flop!
GLUG GLUG GLUG!
YUCK! That smells bad!
It's the sulphur mixing with the other smurf chemicals! It's not dangerous!
PPSSSSHHHH
HEY LOOK! IT'S SMURFING!
Giant carrots! HURRAY! I SUCCEEDED!
Let's run! That carrot is furious!
GRRR
RHAAAA!
Apprentice Smurf made some giant carrots smurf in my garden!
?
You're nothing but a fibber, Farmer Smurf! Your carrots are all itsy-bitsy! Hee hee hee!
As big as this, I tell you, uh huh! We were afraid!
Stop kidding around, Apprentice Smurf!
But it's true, and--
AAAAH HELP!
LOOK!
It's Dopey Smurf!
Did he see some giant carrots, too?!
But it's the truth!
What happened to you, buddy?
BOOHOO-HOOOO... I was bitten by a wild carrot!
© Peyo
2

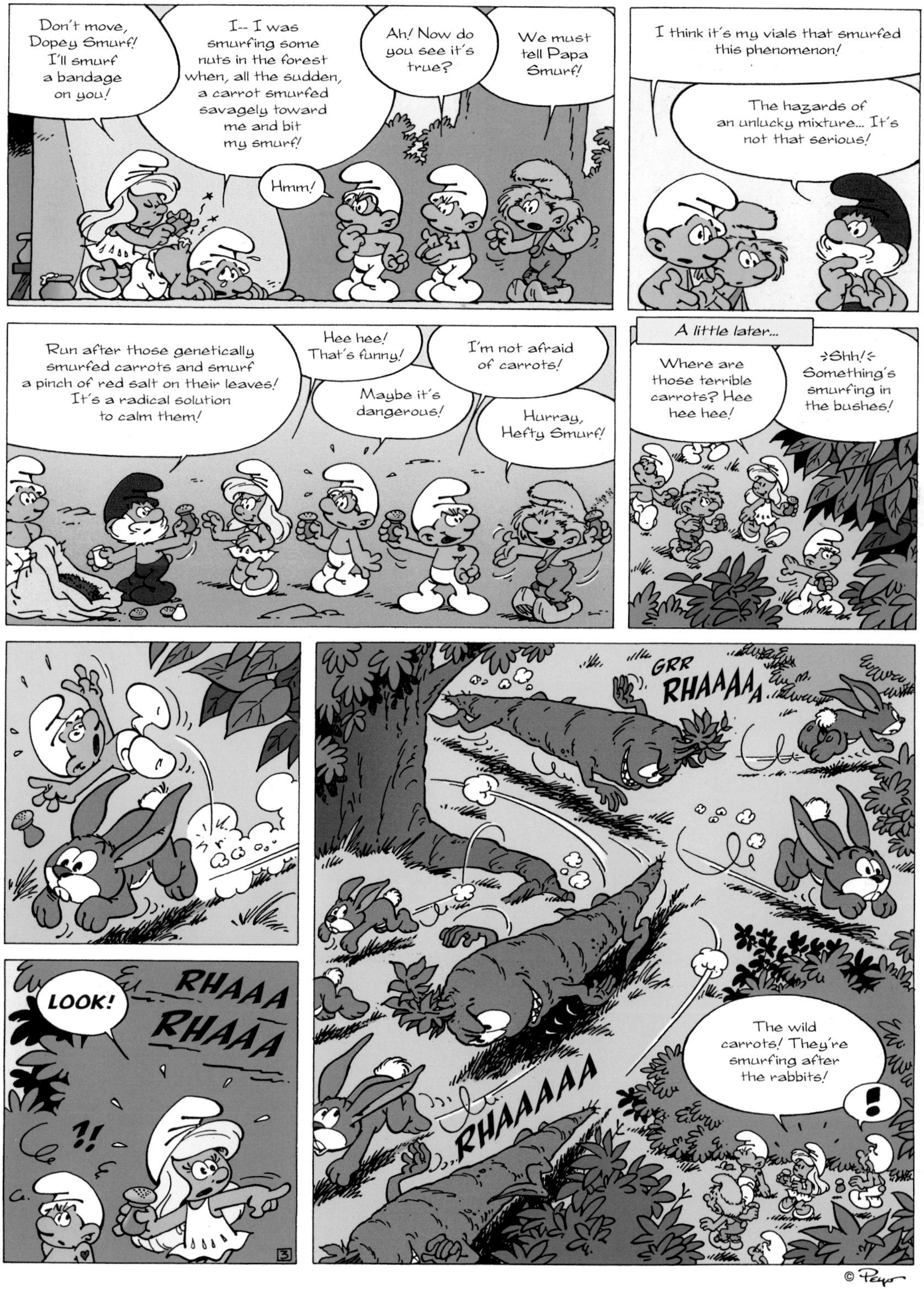
Don't move, Dopey Smurf! I'll smurf a bandage on you!
I-- I was smurfing some nuts in the forest when, all the sudden, a carrot smurfed savagely toward me and bit my smurf!
Hmm!
Ah! Now do you see it's true?
We must tell Papa Smurf!
I think it's my vials that smurfed this phenomenon!
The hazards of an unlucky mixture... It's not that serious!
Run after those genetically smurfed carrots and smurf a pinch of red salt on their leaves! It's a radical solution to calm them!
Hee hee! That's funny!
Maybe it's dangerous!
I'm not afraid of carrots!
Hurray, Hefty Smurf!
A little later...
Where are those terrible carrots? Hee hee hee!
Shh! Something's smurfing in the bushes!
LOOK!
RHAAA
RHAAA
?!
GRR
RHAAAAA
RHAAAAA
The wild carrots! They're smurfing after the rabbits!
!
3
© Peyo

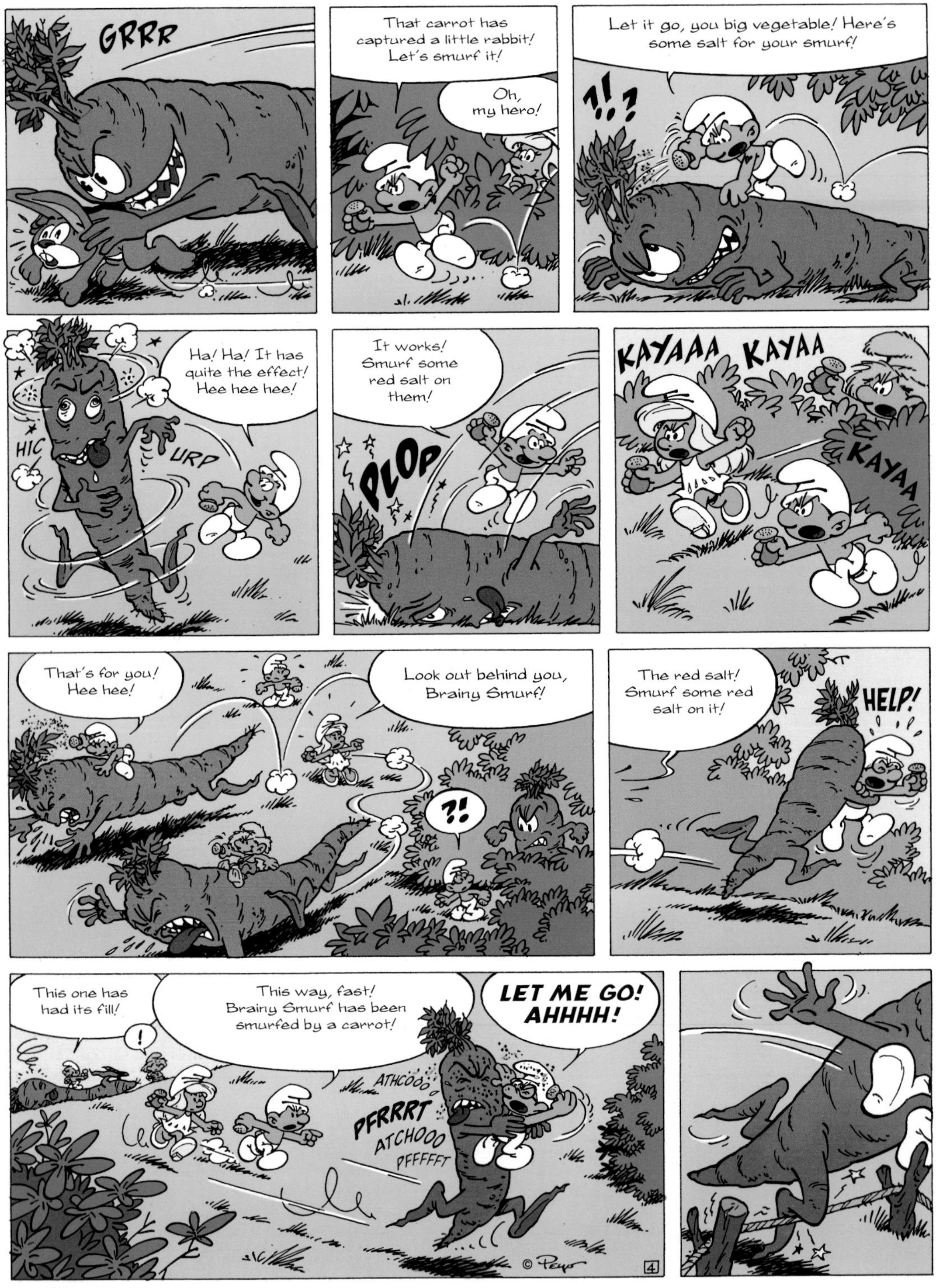
GRRR
That carrot has captured a little rabbit! Let's smurf it!
Oh, my hero!
Let it go, you big vegetable! Here's some salt for your smurf!
?!..?
Ha! Ha! It has quite the effect! Hee hee hee!
HIC
URP
It works! Smurf some red salt on them!
PLOP
KAYAAA KAYAA
KAYAA
That's for you! Hee hee!
Look out behind you, Brainy Smurf!
?!
The red salt! Smurf some red salt on it!
HELP!
This one has had its fill!
!
This way, fast! Brainy Smurf has been smurfed by a carrot!
LET ME GO! AHHHH!
ATHCOOO
PFRRRT
ATCHOOO
PFFFFFT
© Peyo
4

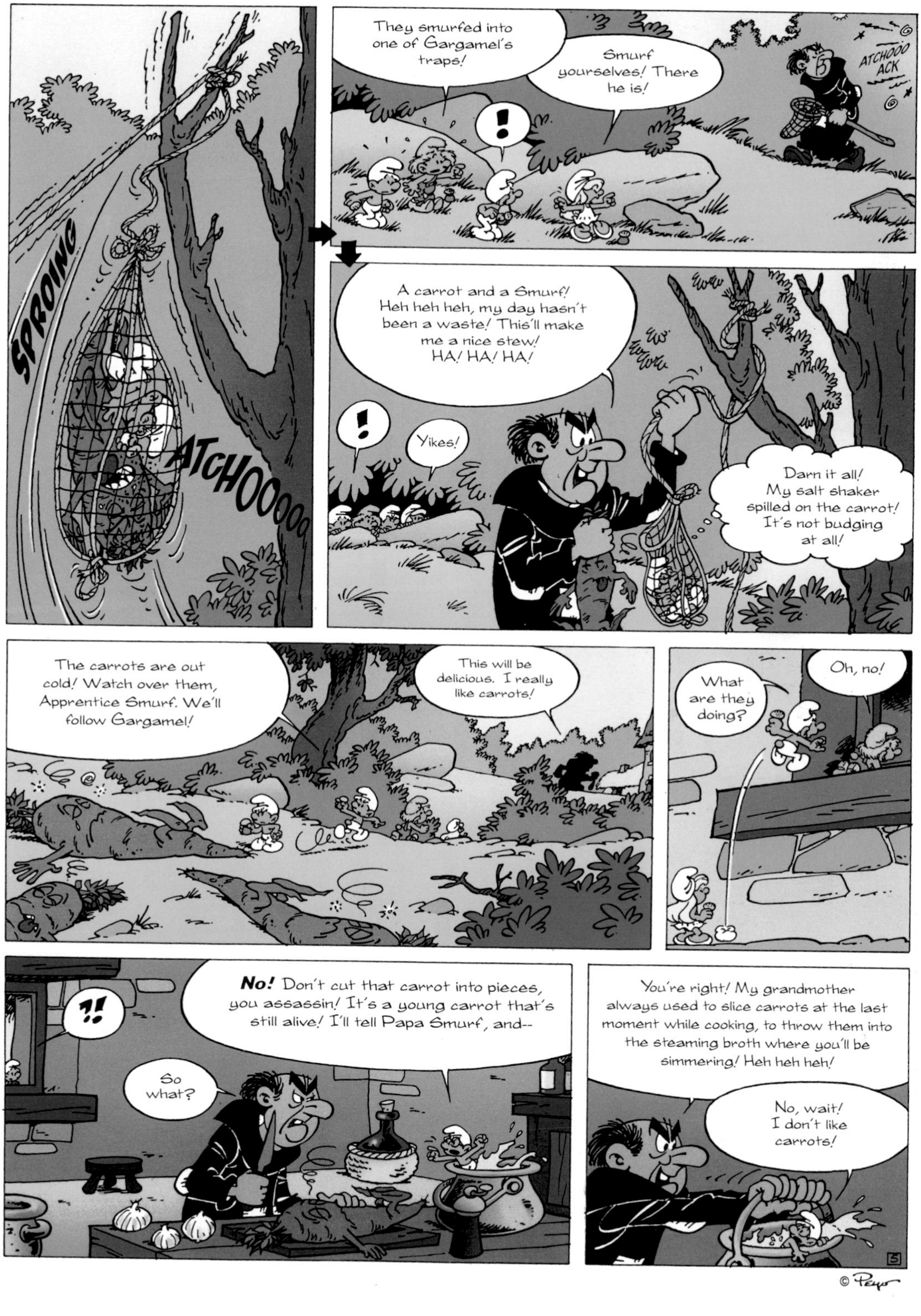
SPROING
ATCHOOOOOO
They smurfed into one of Gargamel's traps!
!
Smurf yourselves! There he is!
ATCHOOO ACK
A carrot and a Smurf! Heh heh heh, my day hasn't been a waste! This'll make me a nice stew! HA! HA! HA!
!
Yikes!
Darn it all! My salt shaker spilled on the carrot! It's not budging at all!
The carrots are out cold! Watch over them, Apprentice Smurf. We'll follow Gargamel!
This will be delicious. I really like carrots!
What are they doing?
Oh, no!
?!
No! Don't cut that carrot into pieces, you assassin! It's a young carrot that's still alive! I'll tell Papa Smurf, and--
So what?
You're right! My grandmother always used to slice carrots at the last moment while cooking, to throw them into the steaming broth where you'll be simmering! Heh heh heh!
No, wait! I don't like carrots!
5
© Peyo

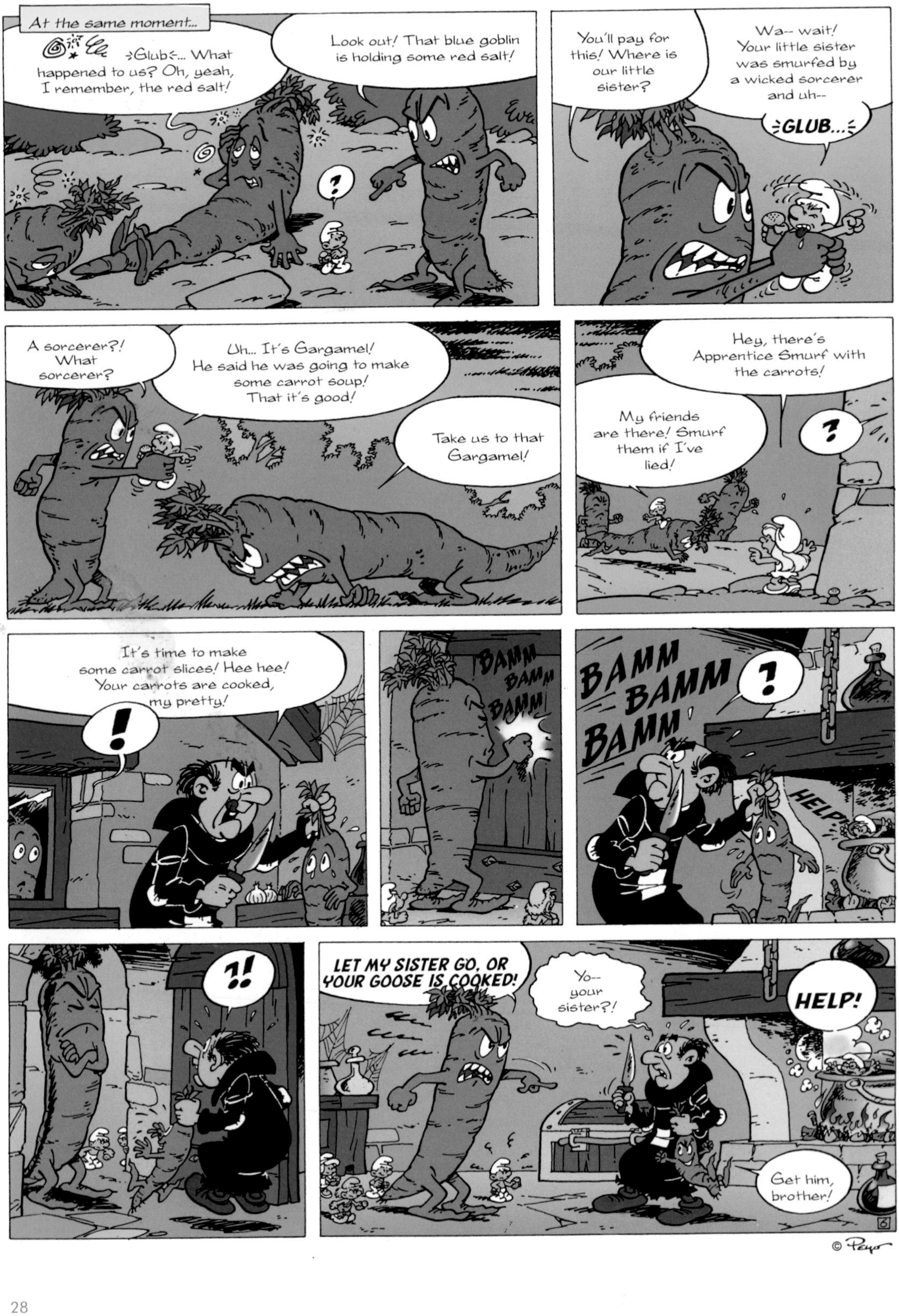
At the same moment...
Glub... What happened to us? Oh, yeah, I remember, the red salt!
Look out! That blue goblin is holding some red salt!
?
You'll pay for this! Where is our little sister?
Wa-- wait! Your little sister was smurfed by a wicked sorcerer and uh--
GLUB...
A sorcerer?! What sorcerer?
Uh... It's Gargamel! He said he was going to make some carrot soup! That it's good!
Take us to that Gargamel!
Hey, there's Apprentice Smurf with the carrots!
My friends are there! Smurf them if I've lied!
?
It's time to make some carrot slices! Hee hee! Your carrots are cooked, my pretty!
!
BAMM BAMM BAMM
BAMM BAMM BAMM
?
HELP!
?!
LET MY SISTER GO, OR YOUR GOOSE IS COOKED!
Yo-- your sister?!
HELP!
Get him, brother!
6
© Peyo

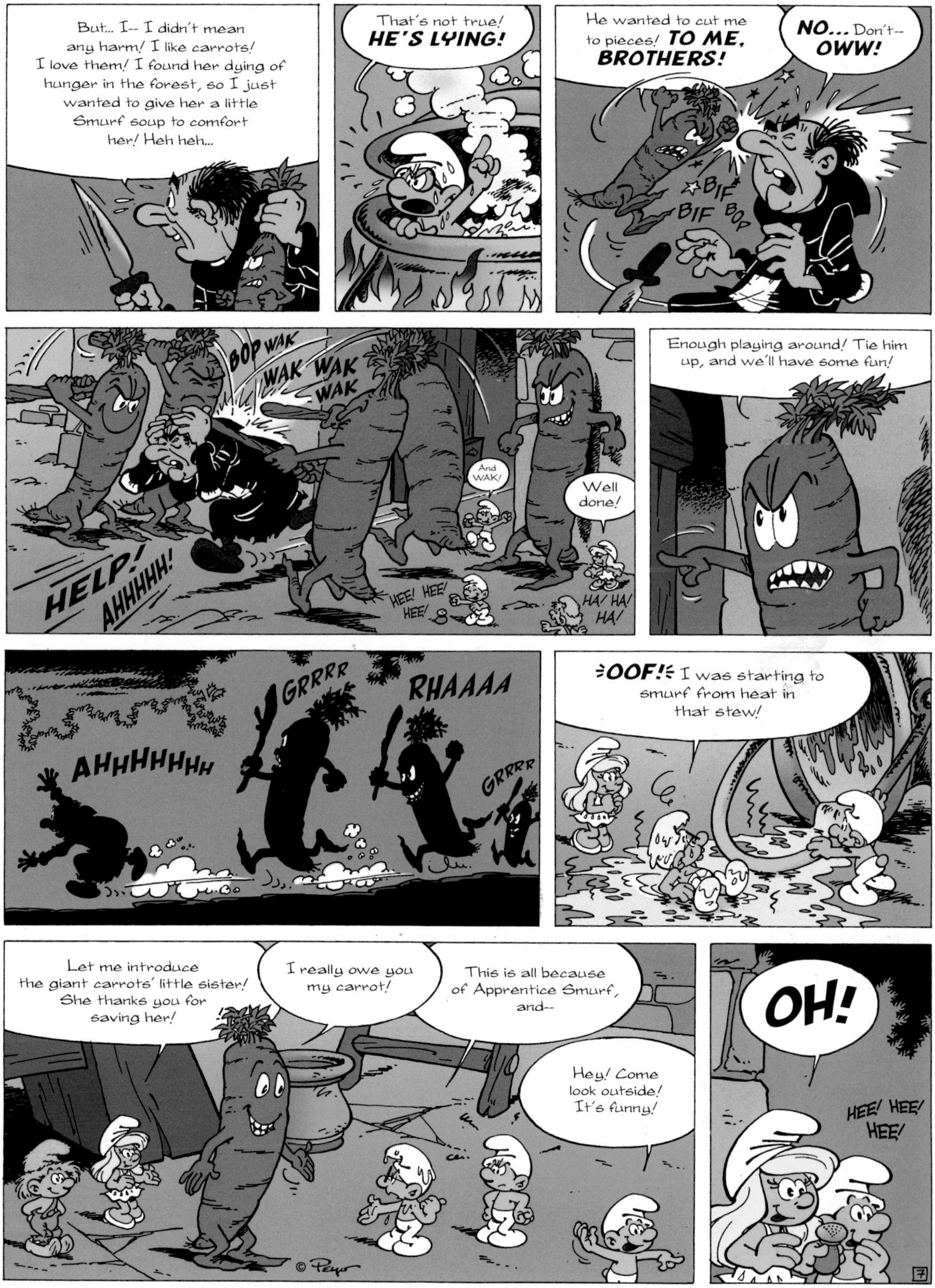
But... I-- I didn't mean any harm! I like carrots! I love them! I found her dying of hunger in the forest, so I just wanted to give her a little Smurf soup to comfort her! Heh heh...
That's not true! HE'S LYING!
He wanted to cut me to pieces! TO ME, BROTHERS!
NO... Don't-- OWW!
BIF BIF BOP
BOP WAK WAK WAK WAK
And WAK!
Well done!
HELP! AHHHHH!
HEE! HEE! HEE!
HA! HA! HA!
Enough playing around! Tie him up, and we'll have some fun!
GRRRR
RHAAAA
AHHHHHHH
GRRRR
OOF! I was starting to smurf from heat in that stew!
Let me introduce the giant carrots' little sister! She thanks you for saving her!
I really owe you my carrot!
This is all because of Apprentice Smurf, and--
Hey! Come look outside! It's funny!
© Peyo
OH!
HEE! HEE! HEE!
7

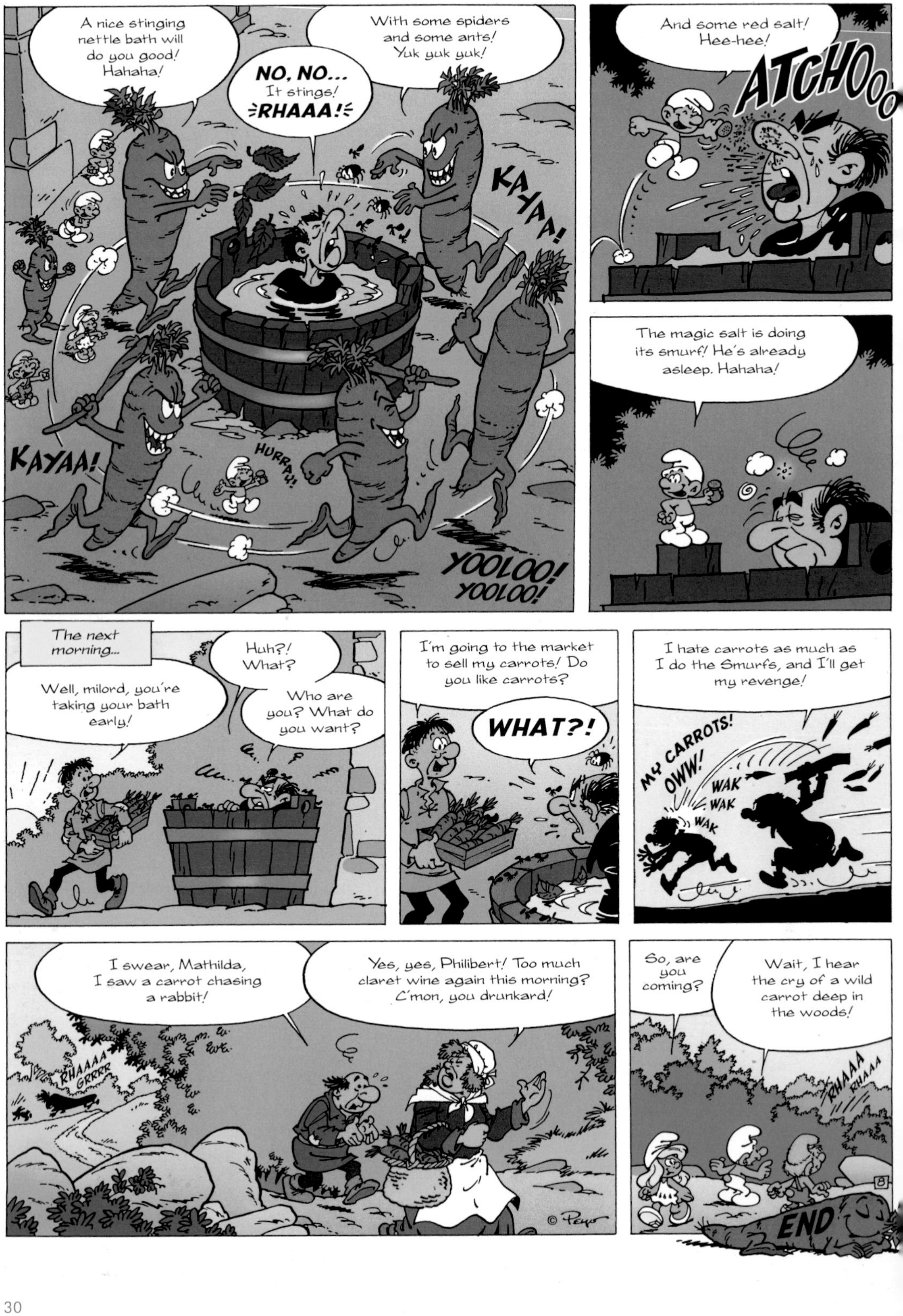
A nice stinging nettle bath will do you good! Hahaha!
NO, NO... It stings! RHAAA!
With some spiders and some ants! Yuk yuk yuk!
KAYAA!
KAYAA!
HURRAH!
YOOLOO! YOOLOO!
And some red salt! Hee-hee!
ATCHOOOO
The magic salt is doing its smurf! He's already asleep. Hahaha!
The next morning...
Well, milord, you're taking your bath early!
Huh?! What?
Who are you? What do you want?
I'm going to the market to sell my carrots! Do you like carrots?
WHAT?!
I hate carrots as much as I do the Smurfs, and I'll get my revenge!
MY CARROTS!
OWW!
WAK
WAK
WAK
I swear, Mathilda, I saw a carrot chasing a rabbit!
Yes, yes, Philibert! Too much claret wine again this morning? C'mon, you drunkard!
RHAAAA GRRRR
© Peyo
So, are you coming?
Wait, I hear the cry of a wild carrot deep in the woods!
RHAAAA RHAAAA
END

THE ICE CASTLE

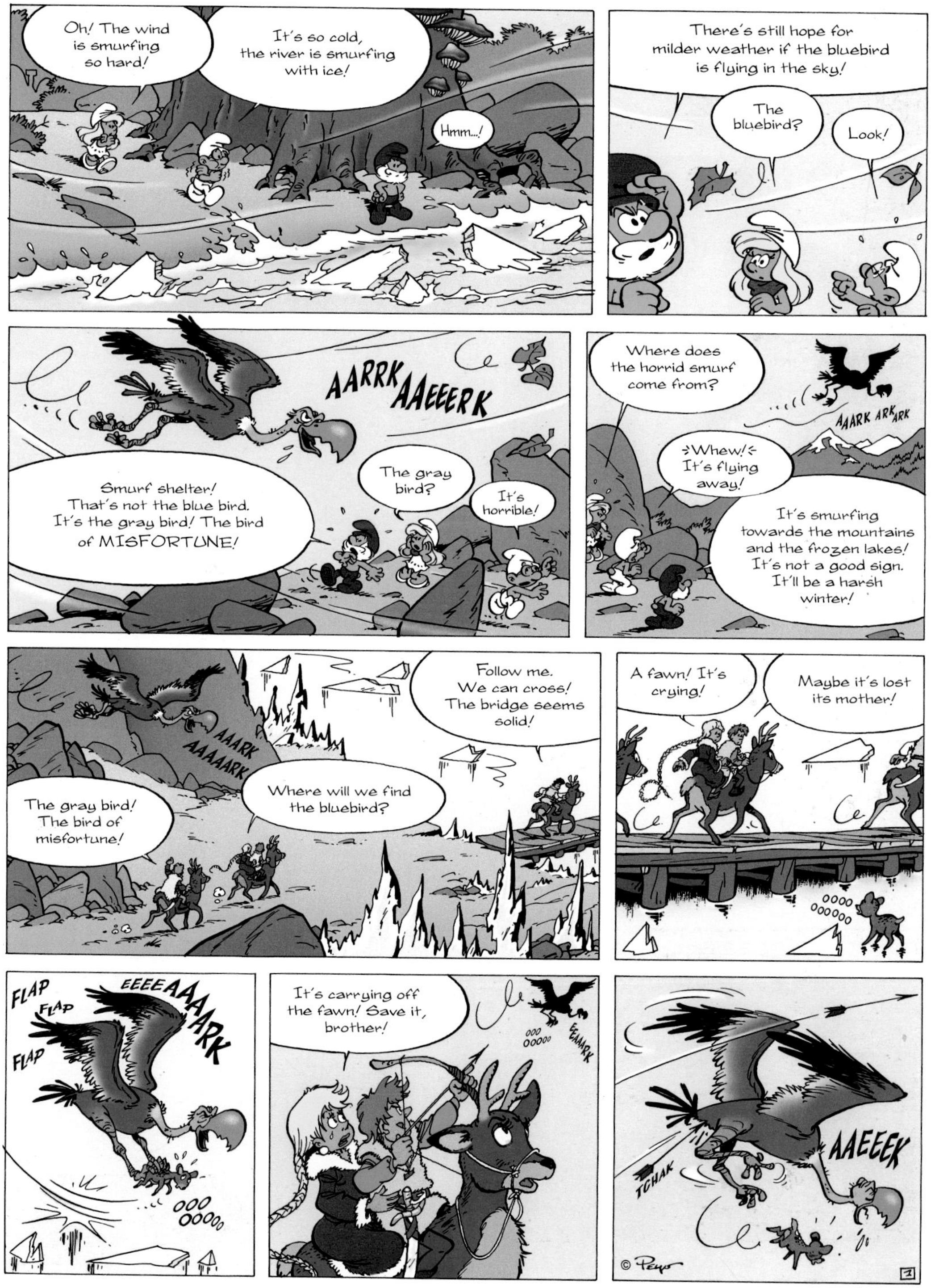

Oh! The wind is smurfing so hard!
It's so cold, the river is smurfing with ice!
Hmm...!
There's still hope for milder weather if the bluebird is flying in the sky!
The bluebird?
Look!
AARRK AAEEERK
Smurf shelter! That's not the blue bird. It's the gray bird! The bird of MISFORTUNE!
The gray bird?
It's horrible!
Where does the horrid smurf come from?
AARK ARK ARK
Whew! It's flying away!
It's smurfing towards the mountains and the frozen lakes! It's not a good sign. It'll be a harsh winter!
AAARK AAAAARK
The gray bird! The bird of misfortune!
Where will we find the bluebird?
Follow me. We can cross! The bridge seems solid!
A fawn! It's crying!
Maybe it's lost its mother!
OOOO OOOOOO
FLAP FLAP FLAP
EEEEAAAARK
OOO OOOOO
It's carrying off the fawn! Save it, brother!
OOO OOOOO
EEAAARK
TCHAK
AAEEEK
© Peyo
1

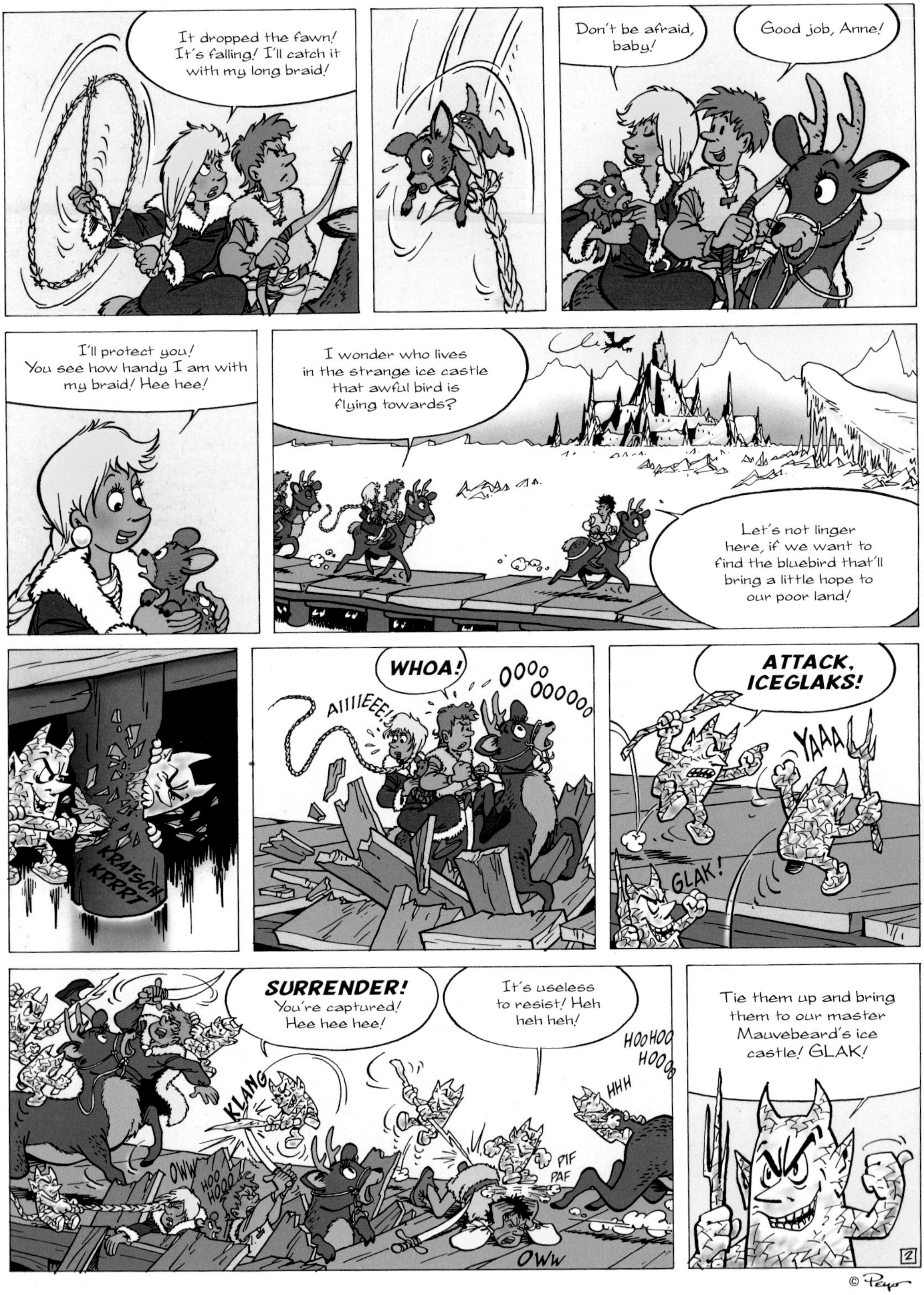
It dropped the fawn! It's falling! I'll catch it with my long braid!
Don't be afraid, baby!
Good job, Anne!
I'll protect you! You see how handy I am with my braid! Hee hee!
I wonder who lives in the strange ice castle that awful bird is flying towards?
Let's not linger here, if we want to find the bluebird that'll bring a little hope to our poor land!
KRATSCH
KRRRT
WHOA!
AIIIIEEE!
OOOO OOOOOO
ATTACK, ICEGLAKS!
YAAA
GLAK!
SURRENDER! You're captured! Hee hee hee!
It's useless to resist! Heh heh heh!
HOO HOO HOO
HHH
KLANG
OWW
HOO HOO
PIF PAF
OWW
Tie them up and bring them to our master Mauvebeard's ice castle! GLAK!
2

© Peyo

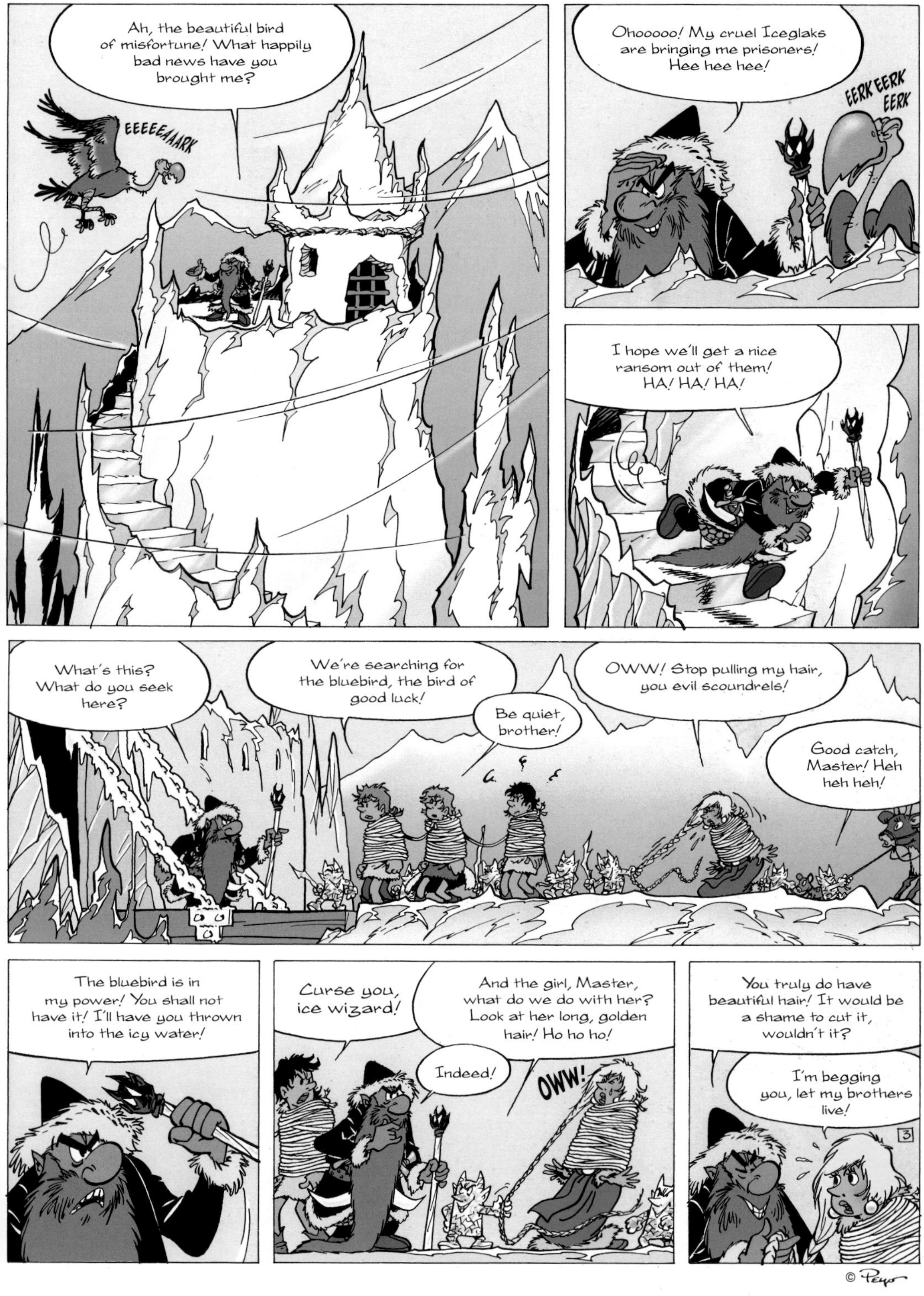
Ah, the beautiful bird of misfortune! What happily bad news have you brought me?
EEEEEAAARK
Ohooooo! My cruel Iceglaks are bringing me prisoners! Hee hee hee!
EERK EERK EERK
I hope we'll get a nice ransom out of them! HA! HA! HA!
What's this? What do you seek here?
We're searching for the bluebird, the bird of good luck!
Be quiet, brother!
OWW! Stop pulling my hair, you evil scoundrels!
Good catch, Master! Heh heh heh!
The bluebird is in my power! You shall not have it! I'll have you thrown into the icy water!
Curse you, ice wizard!
And the girl, Master, what do we do with her? Look at her long, golden hair! Ho ho ho!
Indeed!
OWW!
You truly do have beautiful hair! It would be a shame to cut it, wouldn't it?
I'm begging you, let my brothers live!
3
© Peyo

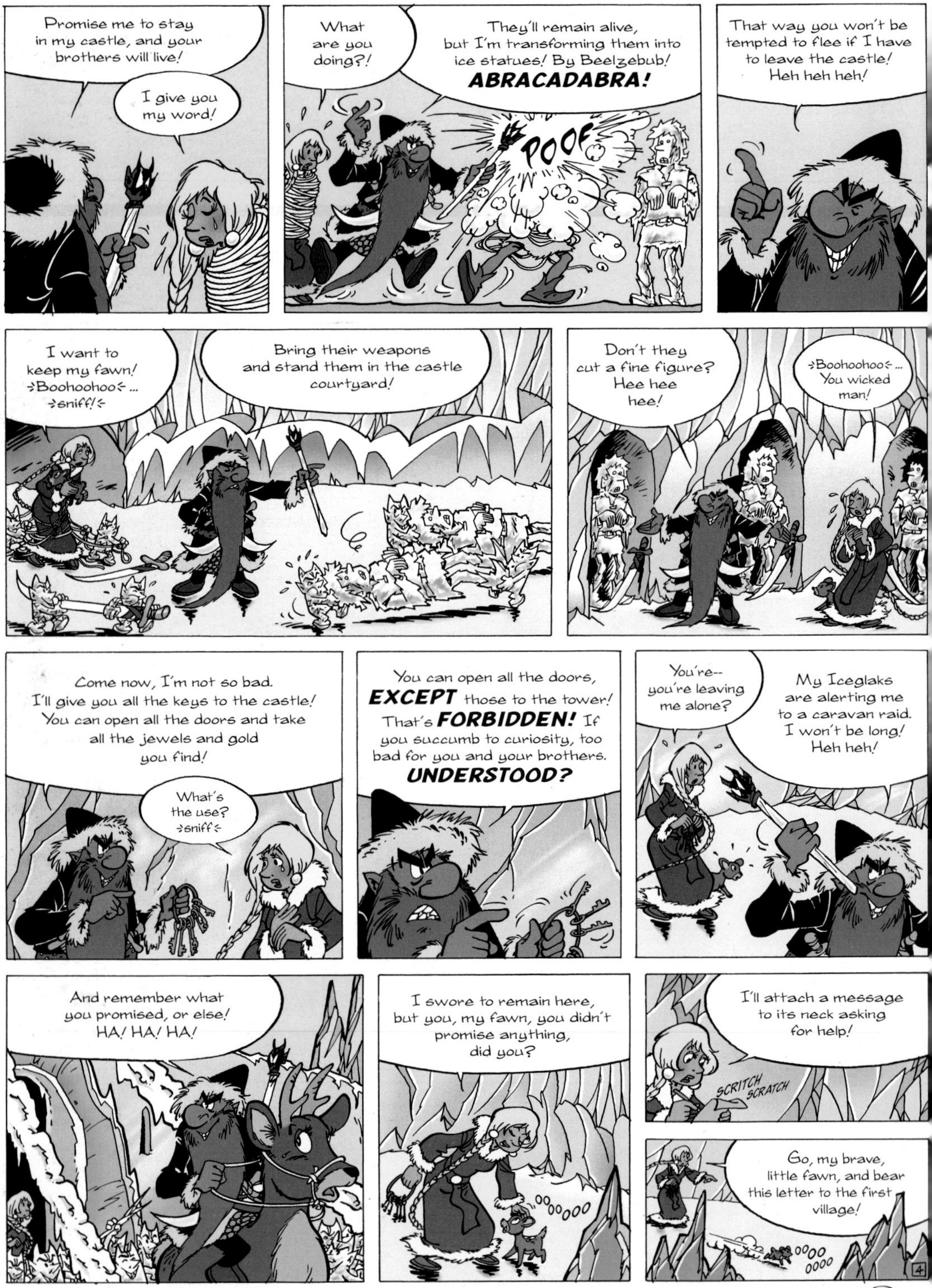
Promise me to stay in my castle, and your brothers will live!
I give you my word!
What are you doing?!
They'll remain alive, but I'm transforming them into ice statues! By Beelzebub! ABRACADABRA!
POOF
That way you won't be tempted to flee if I have to leave the castle! Heh heh heh!
I want to keep my fawn! >Boohoohoo< ... >sniff!<
Bring their weapons and stand them in the castle courtyard!
Don't they cut a fine figure? Hee hee hee!
>Boohoohoo< ... You wicked man!
Come now, I'm not so bad. I'll give you all the keys to the castle! You can open all the doors and take all the jewels and gold you find!
What's the use? >sniff<
You can open all the doors, EXCEPT those to the tower! That's FORBIDDEN! If you succumb to curiosity, too bad for you and your brothers. UNDERSTOOD?
You're-- you're leaving me alone?
My Iceglaks are alerting me to a caravan raid. I won't be long! Heh heh!
And remember what you promised, or else! HA! HA! HA!
I swore to remain here, but you, my fawn, you didn't promise anything, did you?
OOOOOO
I'll attach a message to its neck asking for help!
SCRITCH SCRATCH
Go, my brave, little fawn, and bear this letter to the first village!
OOOOOOO
4

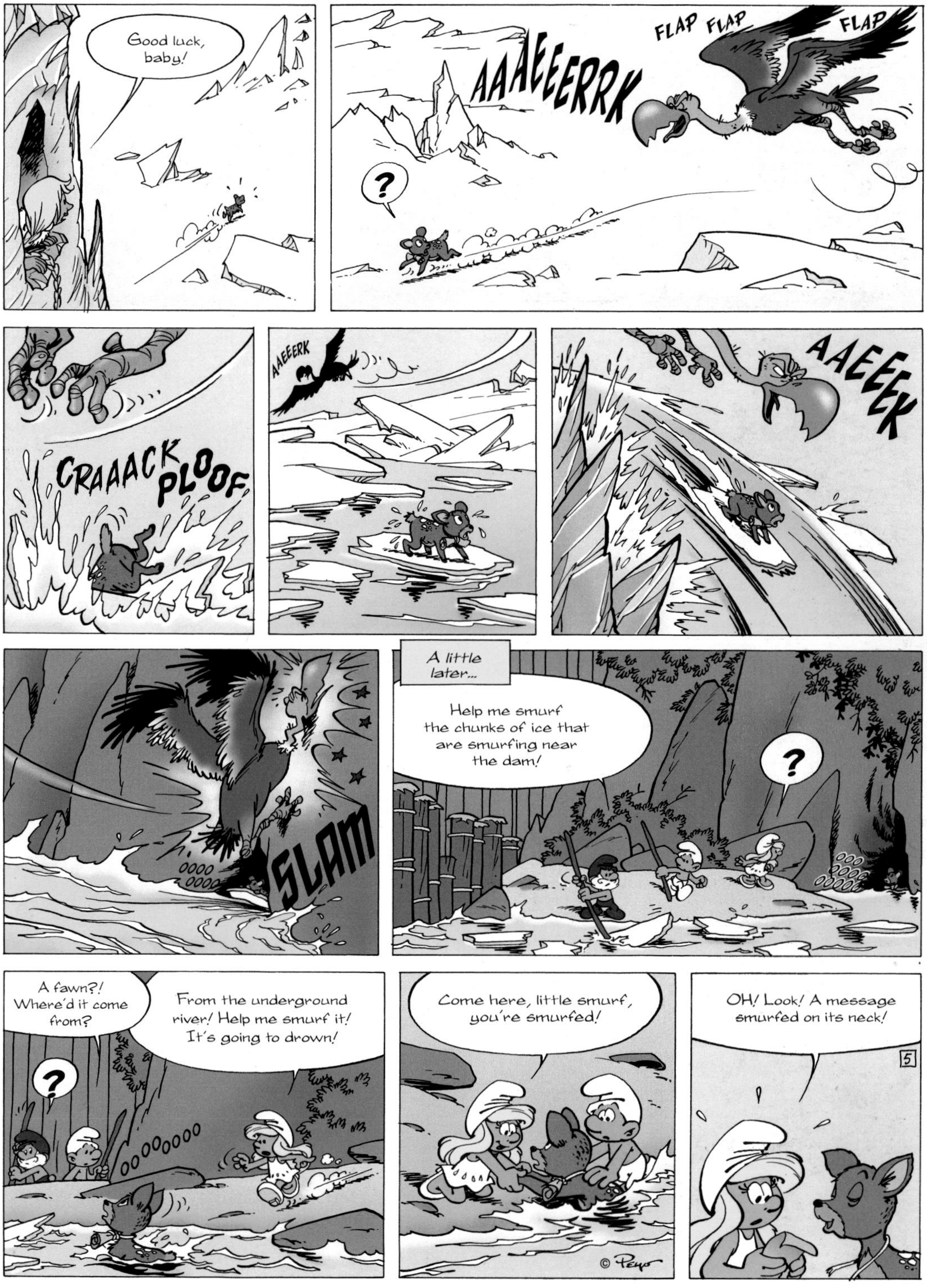
Good luck, baby!
AAAEEERRK
FLAP FLAP FLAP
?
CRAAACK PLOOF
AAEEERK
AAEEEK
SLAM
oooo oooo
A little later...
Help me smurf the chunks of ice that are smurfing near the dam!
?
oooo oooooo
A fawn?! Where'd it come from?
From the underground river! Help me smurf it! It's going to drown!
?
oooOOOOO
Come here, little smurf, you're smurfed!
© Peyo
OH! Look! A message smurfed on its neck!
5

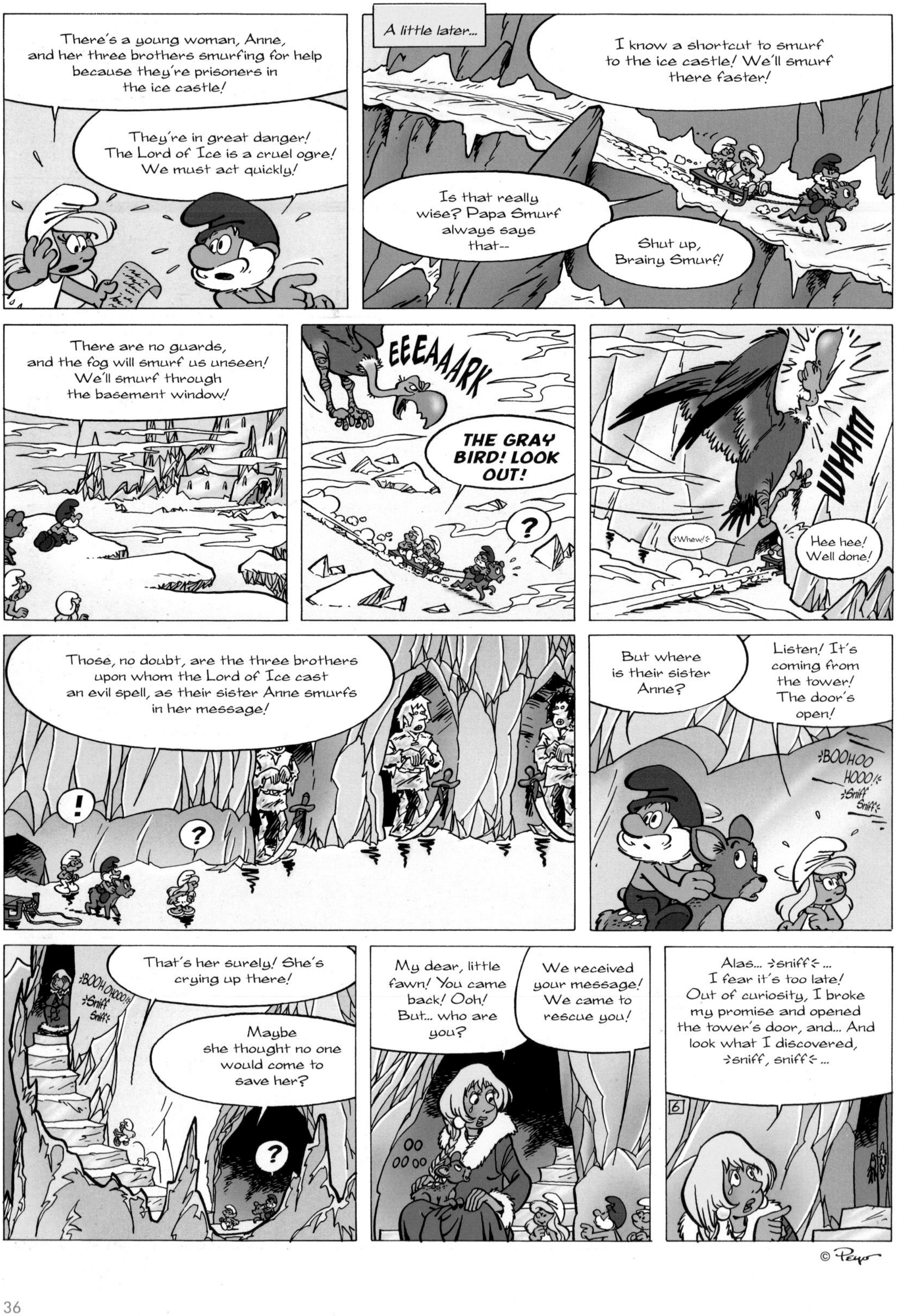
There's a young woman, Anne, and her three brothers smurfing for help because they're prisoners in the ice castle!
They're in great danger! The Lord of Ice is a cruel ogre! We must act quickly!
A little later...
I know a shortcut to smurf to the ice castle! We'll smurf there faster!
Is that really wise? Papa Smurf always says that--
Shut up, Brainy Smurf!
There are no guards, and the fog will smurf us unseen! We'll smurf through the basement window!
EEEAAARK
THE GRAY BIRD! LOOK OUT!
?
WHAM
Whew!
Hee hee! Well done!
Those, no doubt, are the three brothers upon whom the Lord of Ice cast an evil spell, as their sister Anne smurfs in her message!
!
?
But where is their sister Anne?
Listen! It's coming from the tower! The door's open!
BOOHOO HOOO!
Sniff Sniff
That's her surely! She's crying up there!
BOOHOOOO!
Sniff Sniff
Maybe she thought no one would come to save her?
?
My dear, little fawn! You came back! Ooh! But... who are you?
We received your message! We came to rescue you!
Alas... sniff ... I fear it's too late! Out of curiosity, I broke my promise and opened the tower's door, and... And look what I discovered, sniff, sniff ...
6

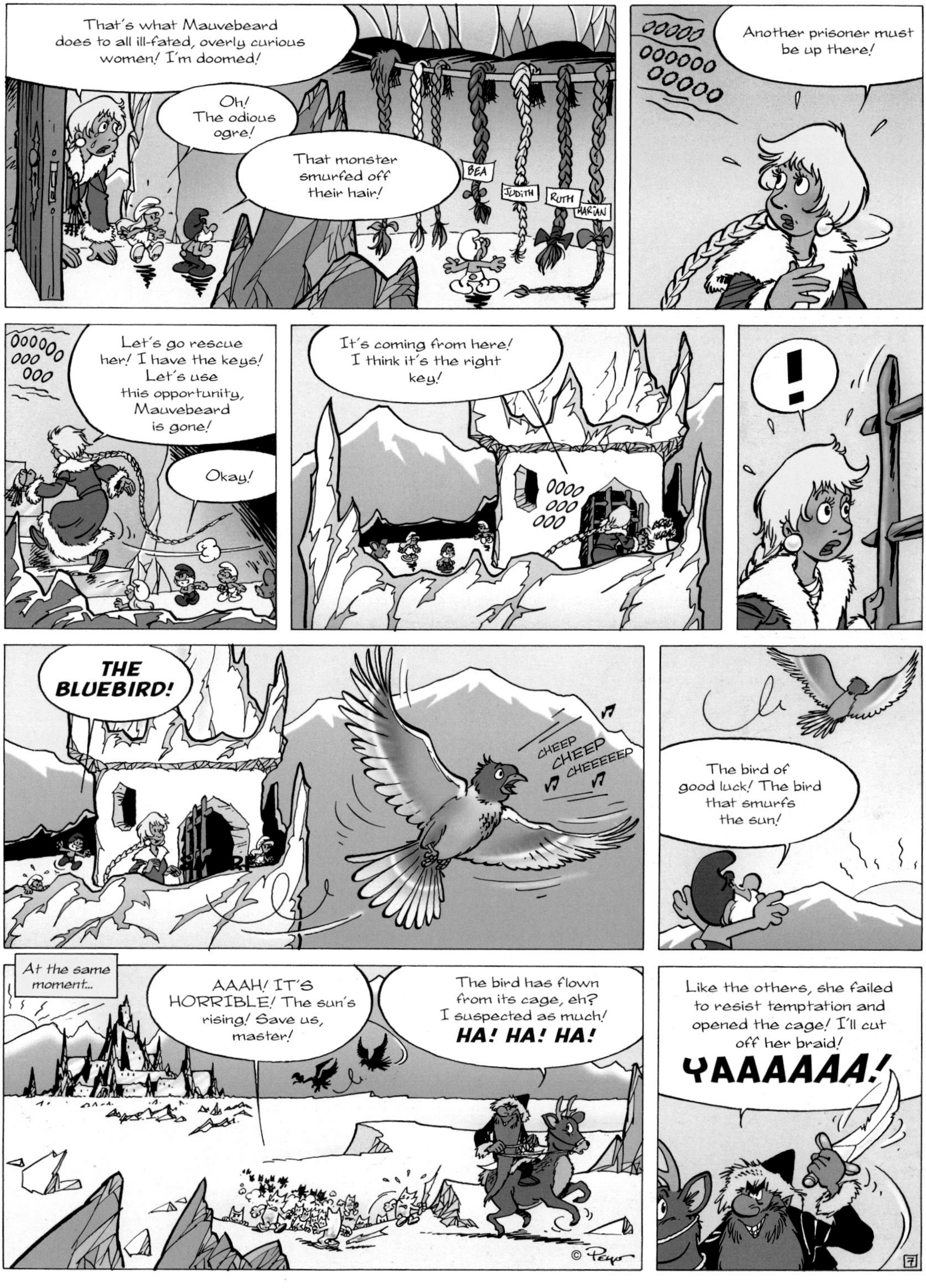

That's what Mauvebeard does to all ill-fated, overly curious women! I'm doomed!
Oh! The odious ogre!
That monster smurfed off their hair!
BEA
JUDITH
RUTH
MARIAN
OOOOO OOOOOO OOOOO
Another prisoner must be up there!
OOOOOO OOO OOO
Let's go rescue her! I have the keys! Let's use this opportunity, Mauvebeard is gone!
Okay!
It's coming from here! I think it's the right key!
OOOO OOO OOO
!
THE BLUEBIRD!
CHEEP CHEEP CHEEEEEP
The bird of good luck! The bird that smurfs the sun!
At the same moment...
AAAH! IT'S HORRIBLE! The sun's rising! Save us, master!
The bird has flown from its cage, eh? I suspected as much! HA! HA! HA!
© Peyo
Like the others, she failed to resist temptation and opened the cage! I'll cut off her braid!
YAAAAAA!
7

The sun is melting the ice!

And my brothers? Let's go down quick!

?

I'LL CUT OFF YOUR BRAID! HA! HA! HA!

Come get it, if you dare, you hairy old ogre!

Ah, the traitor!

Leave him to us. We'll cut off his beard!

Yeah!

HA! HA! HA!

The spell is broken! You're alive! The ice melted!

?!!

YAAAAA

NO! Not my beard! MERCY! ⸘ARGH!⸘

SLICE

RHAAA! Run for your lives!

HA! HA! HA! They're melting in the sun! Smurf them!

BOO

ARG

SPLASH

May the bluebird smurf good weather to your country, my friends!

Thank you, kind, blue elf!

HELP! I CAN'T SWIM! I'LL AVENGE MYSELF!

Could you smurf me a big favor when から the langue....

Oh, yes! Hee hee hee!

Farewell, friends!

So, are you coming, sister?

Wait! She's smurfing me a braid!

END

38

Welcome to the super-scary SMURFS MONSTERS graphic novel from Papercutz, the not-at-all scary company dedicated to publishing great graphic novels for all ages. I'm Jim Salicrup, the Papa Smurf lookalike who is the Smurf-in-Chief, here to bring you up-to-date on all our latest Smurfy plans…

The Smurfs began over fifty years ago, as comics characters created by Pierre Culliford, better known as Peyo, for a story starring *Johan and Peewit*. The audience immediately embraced The Smurfs (originally, and still known in France and Belgium, as the Schtroumpfs), which soon led to them getting their own ongoing series of graphic novels. Movies, toys, cartoons, and much, much more followed, and the Smurfs became superstars. The Smurfs didn't hit the U.S. until the 80s when their hit animated Saturday morning TV series started its 9-year successful run. While there were a few reprints of the original SMURFS graphic novels published in the U.S., they were published mainly as TV tie-ins designed to cash in on THE SMURFS "fad."

When Papercutz was founded ten years ago by publisher Terry Nantier and me, we dreamed of publishing THE SMURFS, one of the all-time great classic series of graphic novels for all ages. Things actually worked out even better than we hoped, as we've not only been publishing THE SMURFS in several different formats, but we've also been fortunate enough to publish other Peyo characters as well! For example…

PUSSYCAT – a single deluxe volume, collecting all of the Pussycat comic strips by Peyo! Yes, before Azrael, Peyo created this charming cat comic strip that ran for many years, but had never been published in the U.S. before.

THE SMURFS ANTHOLOGY – An ongoing deluxe format graphic novel series, presenting Peyo's SMURFS in the size at which they were originally published. This series also features the *Johan and Peewit* stories that originally featured THE SMURFS. Johan is a page in the royal court, and Peewit is the jester. Together they're great friends and courageous adventurers. Plus, our very own Smurfologist Matt. Murray supplies insightful introductions, offering a fascinating historic perspective to the material.

THE SMURFS AND FRIENDS – Similar to the THE SMURFS ANTHOLOGY in many ways, this deluxe format graphic novel series collects THE SMURFS comics strips, the Smurfless *Johan and Peewit* stories, and BENNY BREAKIRON, Peyo's pint-size super-hero, who is a very nice five year-old French boy with unbelievable power, except when he gets a cold. And there are even more fact-filled introductions by Matt. Murray, who puts it all in proper Smurfic context.

Which brings us back to SMURFS MONSTERS, our third SMURFS special, following THE SMURFS CHRISTMAS and FOREVER SMURFETTE. These special themed graphic novels have proven quite popular. While the Smurfs have faced many scary creatures in the past, apart from their arch foe Gargamel, including Bigmouth the Ogre, never have they ever faced so many monsters all in just one graphic novel! But as scary as these monsters can be, and as horrible as their goals are, there's still something kind of funny about all of them! I mean, monster carrots? Truly, these are monsters to laugh with… or at!

We hope you enjoy this SMURFS special, and don't forget about the regular THE SMURFS series—that's where all the Smurftastic fun began!

Smurf you later,

Jim

STAY IN TOUCH!
EMAIL: Salicrup@papercutz.com
WEB: www.papercutz.com
TWITTER: @papercutzgn
FACEBOOK: PAPERCUTZGRAPHICNOVELS
SNAIL MAIL: Papercutz, 160 Broadway,
   Suite 700, East Wing, New York, NY 10038

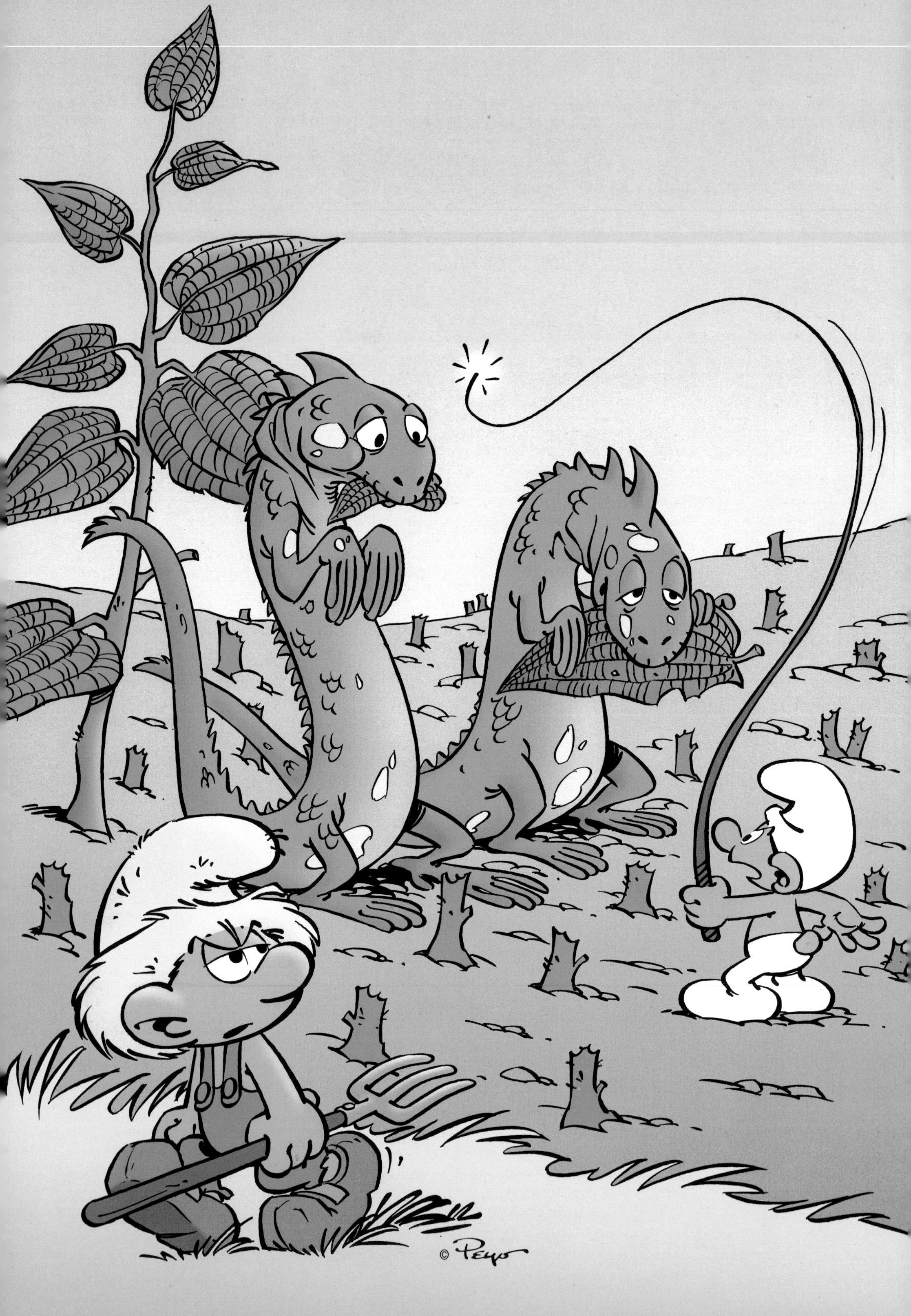
© Peyo

BIGMOUTH AND THE LIZARDS

It's Bigmouth!* He's smurfing to Gargamel's. Smurf yourselves!

?

Bigmouth?

Calm down! We're arriving at Gargamel's, your new master!

GRRGROM NYEEEE GROM

I wonder what he's smurfing in his sack...?

Let's try to find out! Smurf me silently!

Bigmouth, it's you! FINALLY! Did you bring what I asked for?

It's in the bag! Hee hee!

It'd be better to go tell Papa Smurf and--

Wait for me there! I'll go smurf a look inside!

Yes, but--

I fixed you a nice meal, and I'll feed you for a month, as agreed!

YUM! YUM! That smells good. I'M HUNGRY!

?

Uh... May I open the sack?

Be careful, those YUM... Little monsters are very mean!

SLURP YUM GROMP GRAAAAA GROOOO GROM

OH!

*See THE SMURFS#13 "Smurf Soup" for Bigmouth's first Smurfy appearance!

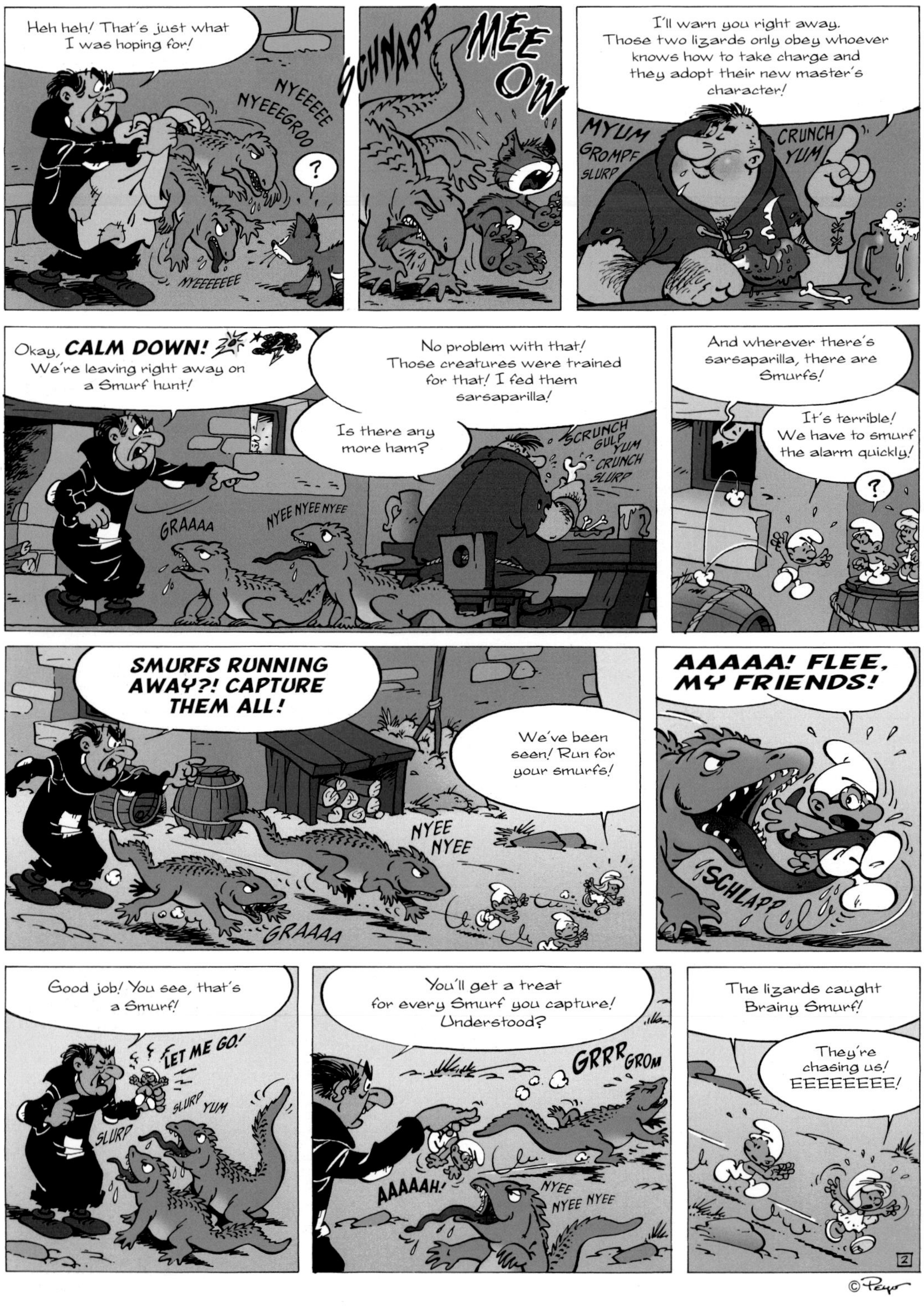
Heh heh! That's just what I was hoping for!
NYEEEEE NYEEEGROO
?
NYEEEEEEE
SCHNAPP
MEE OW
I'll warn you right away. Those two lizards only obey whoever knows how to take charge and they adopt their new master's character!
MYUM GROMPF SLURP
CRUNCH YUM
Okay, CALM DOWN! We're leaving right away on a Smurf hunt!
No problem with that! Those creatures were trained for that! I fed them sarsaparilla!
Is there any more ham?
SCRUNCH GULP YUM CRUNCH SLURP
GRAAAA
NYEE NYEE NYEE
And wherever there's sarsaparilla, there are Smurfs!
It's terrible! We have to smurf the alarm quickly!
?
SMURFS RUNNING AWAY?! CAPTURE THEM ALL!
We've been seen! Run for your smurfs!
NYEE NYEE
GRAAAA
AAAAA! FLEE, MY FRIENDS!
SCHLAPP
Good job! You see, that's a Smurf!
LET ME GO!
SLURP YUM
SLURP
You'll get a treat for every Smurf you capture! Understood?
GRRR GROM
AAAAAH!
NYEE NYEE NYEE
The lizards caught Brainy Smurf!
They're chasing us! EEEEEEEE!
2
© Peyo

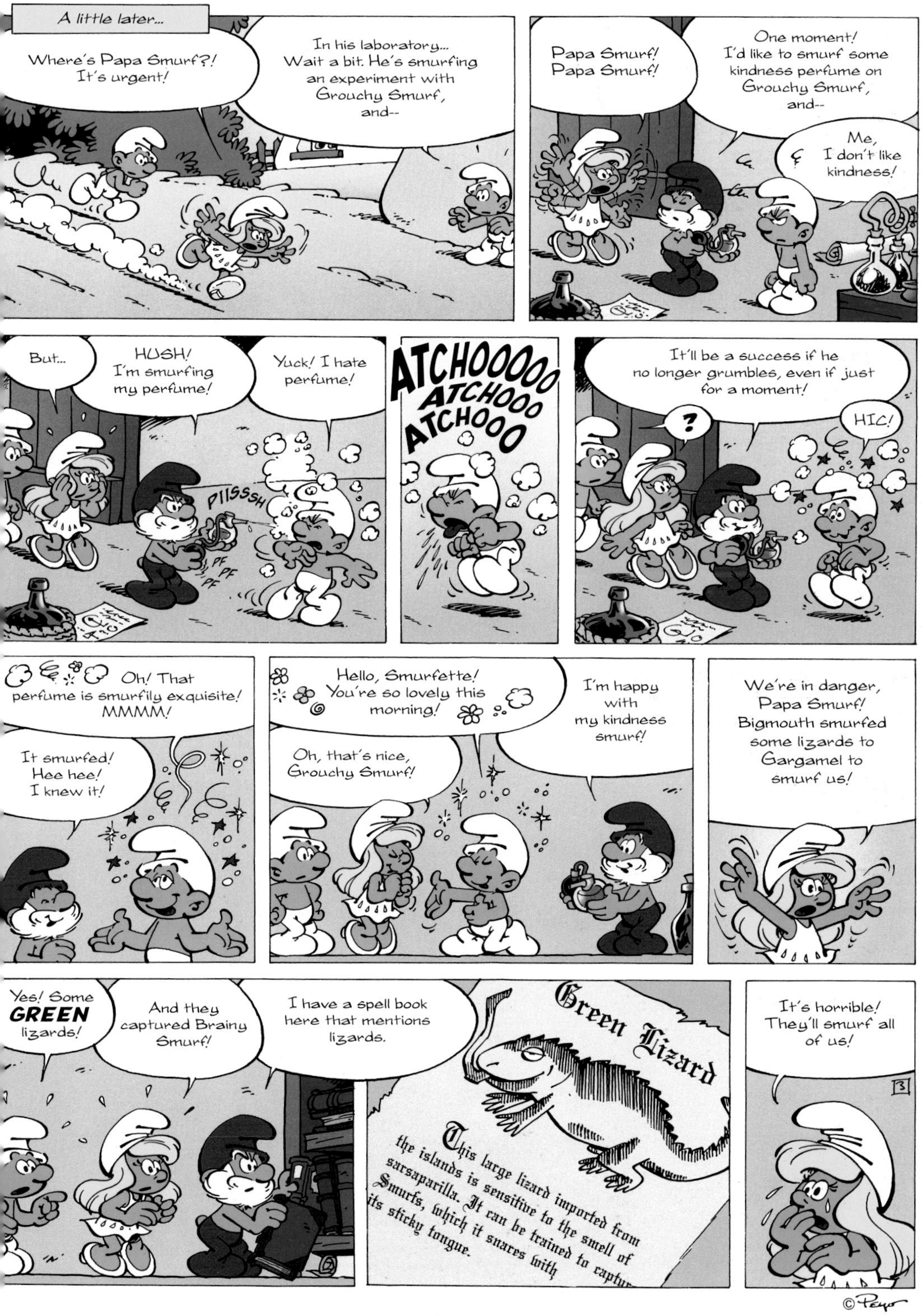
A little later...
Where's Papa Smurf?! It's urgent!
In his laboratory... Wait a bit. He's smurfing an experiment with Grouchy Smurf, and--
Papa Smurf! Papa Smurf!
One moment! I'd like to smurf some kindness perfume on Grouchy Smurf, and--
Me, I don't like kindness!
But...
HUSH! I'm smurfing my perfume!
Yuck! I hate perfume!
PIISSSH
PF PF PF
ATCHOOOOO ATCHOOO ATCHOOO
It'll be a success if he no longer grumbles, even if just for a moment!
?
HIC!
Oh! That perfume is smurfily exquisite! MMMM!
It smurfed! Hee hee! I knew it!
Hello, Smurfette! You're so lovely this morning!
Oh, that's nice, Grouchy Smurf!
I'm happy with my kindness smurf!
We're in danger, Papa Smurf! Bigmouth smurfed some lizards to Gargamel to smurf us!
Yes! Some GREEN lizards!
And they captured Brainy Smurf!
I have a spell book here that mentions lizards.
Green Lizard
This large lizard imported from the islands is sensitive to the smell of sarsaparilla. It can be trained to captur Smurfs, which it snares with its sticky tongue.
It's horrible! They'll smurf all of us!
3
© Peyo

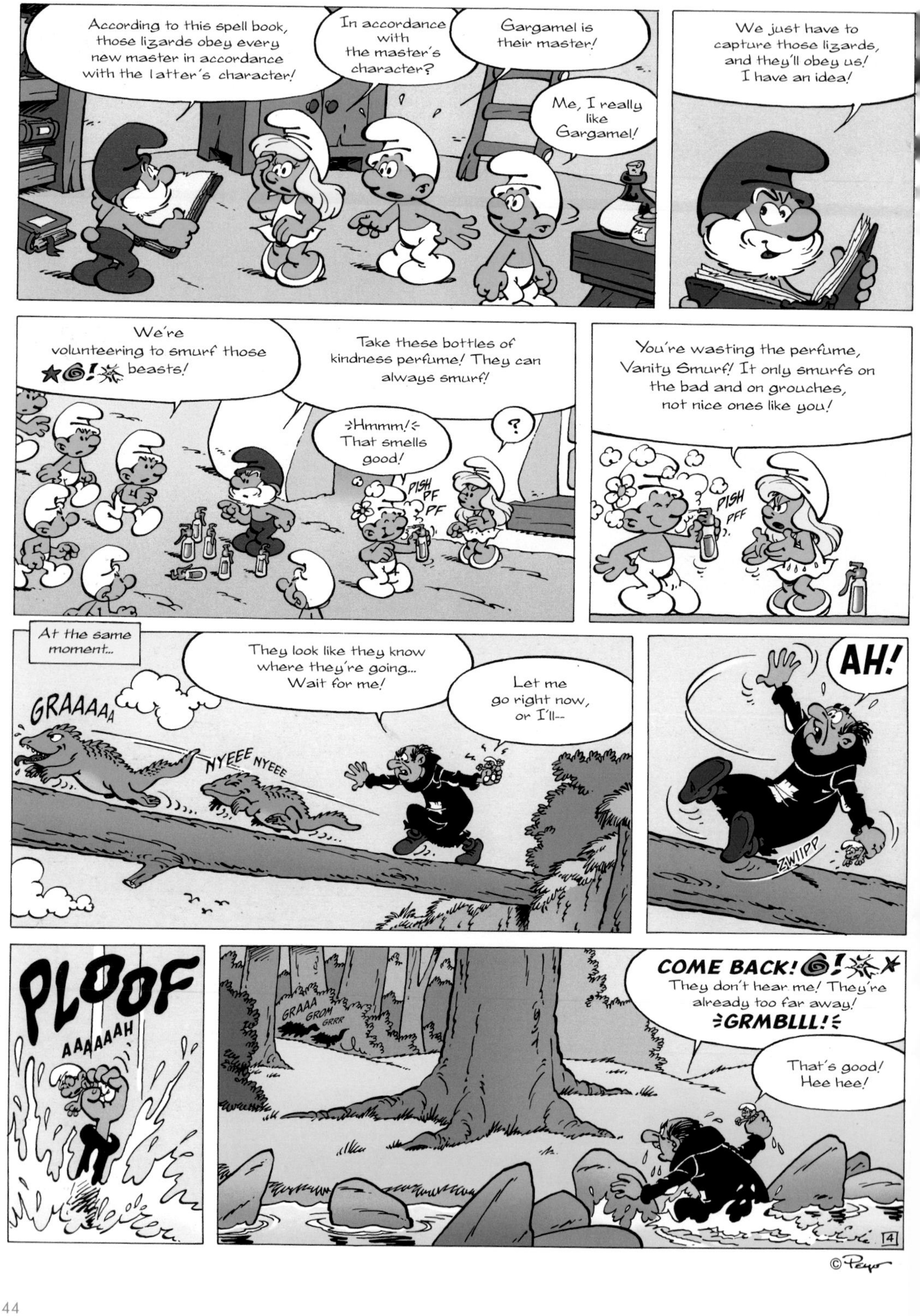
According to this spell book, those lizards obey every new master in accordance with the latter's character!
In accordance with the master's character?
Gargamel is their master!
Me, I really like Gargamel!
We just have to capture those lizards, and they'll obey us! I have an idea!
We're volunteering to smurf those ★@!✷ beasts!
Take these bottles of kindness perfume! They can always smurf!
Hmmm! That smells good!
PISH PF PF
?
You're wasting the perfume, Vanity Smurf! It only smurfs on the bad and on grouches, not nice ones like you!
PISH PFF
At the same moment...
They look like they know where they're going... Wait for me!
GRAAAAA
NYEEE NYEEE
Let me go right now, or I'll--
AH!
ZWIIPP
PLOOF
AAAAAAH
GRAAA GROM GRRR
COME BACK! @!✷✶ They don't hear me! They're already too far away! GRMBLLL!
That's good! Hee hee!
4
© Peyo

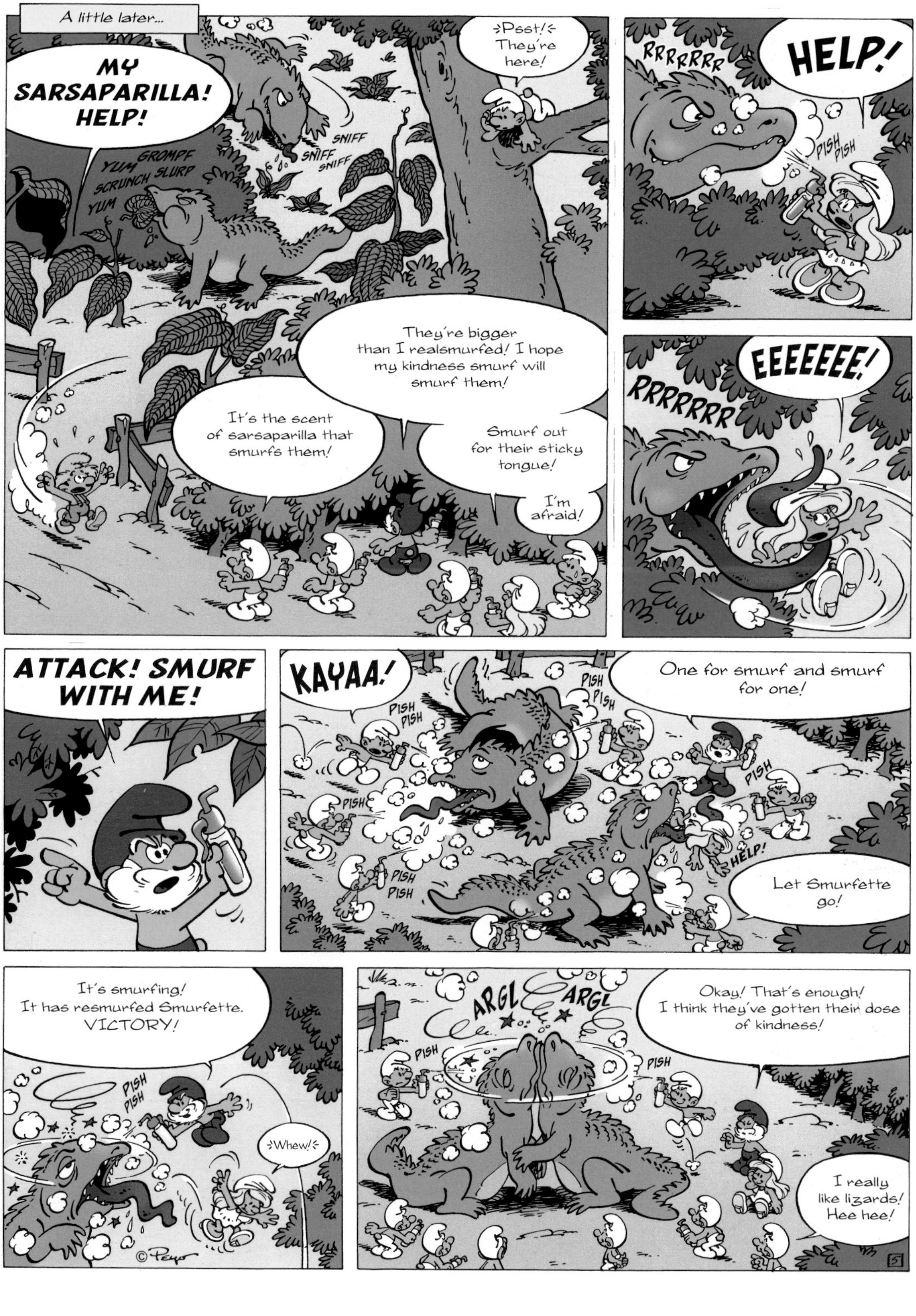
A little later...
MY SARSAPARILLA! HELP!
YUM GROMPF
SCRUNCH SLURP
YUM
SNIFF SNIFF SNIFF
Psst! They're here!
They're bigger than I realsmurfed! I hope my kindness smurf will smurf them!
It's the scent of sarsaparilla that smurfs them!
Smurf out for their sticky tongue!
I'm afraid!
RRRRRRR
HELP!
PISH PISH
RRRRRRR
EEEEEEE!
ATTACK! SMURF WITH ME!
KAYAA!
PISH PISH
One for smurf and smurf for one!
PISH
PISH
HELP!
PISH PISH
Let Smurfette go!
It's smurfing! It has resmurfed Smurfette. VICTORY!
PISH PISH
Whew!
© Peyo
ARGL ARGL
Okay! That's enough! I think they've gotten their dose of kindness!
PISH
PISH
I really like lizards! Hee hee!

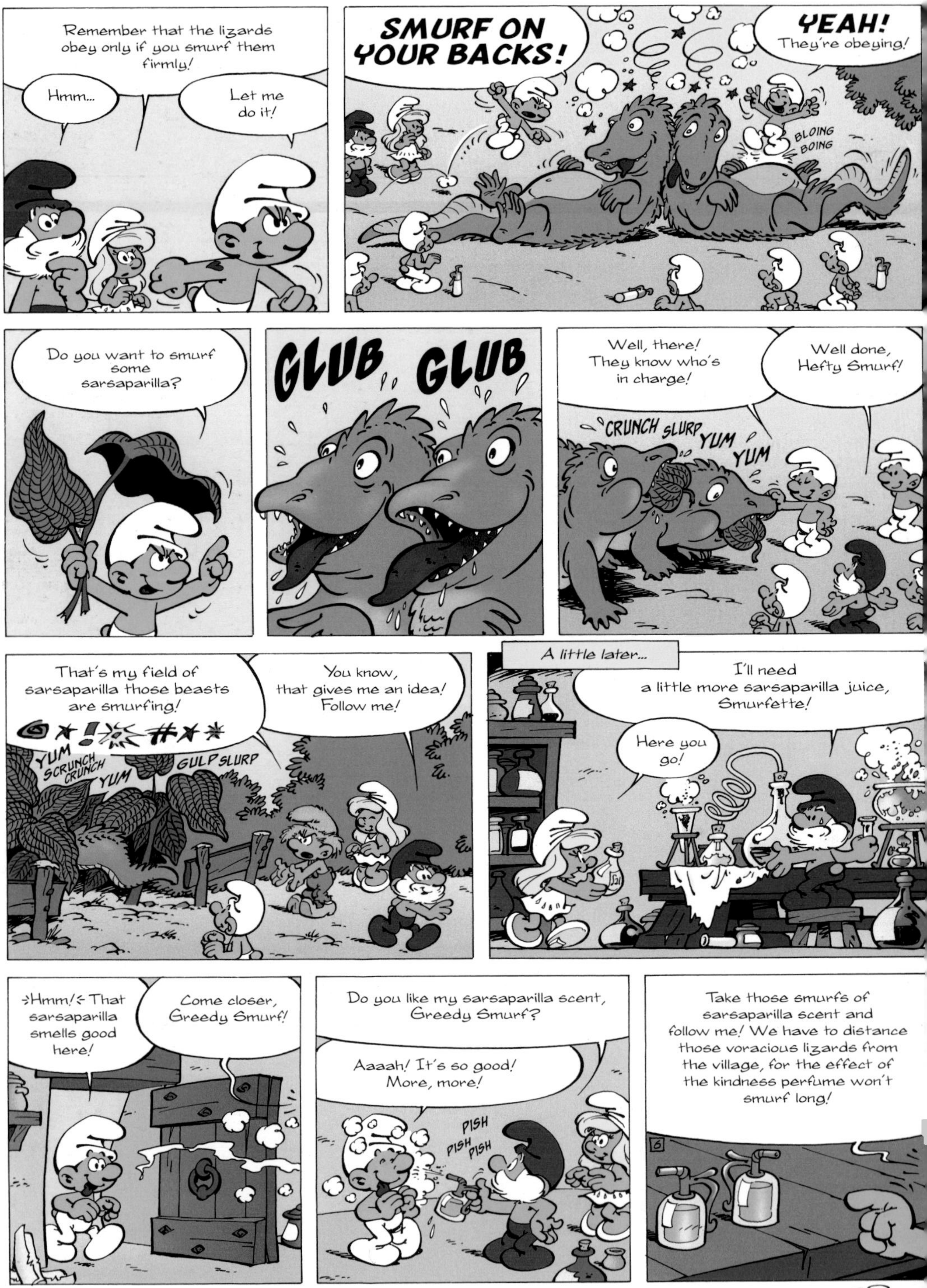

Remember that the lizards obey only if you smurf them firmly!
Hmm...
Let me do it!
SMURF ON YOUR BACKS!
BLOING BOING
YEAH! They're obeying!
Do you want to smurf some sarsaparilla?
GLUB GLUB
Well, there! They know who's in charge!
Well done, Hefty Smurf!
CRUNCH SLURP YUM YUM
That's my field of sarsaparilla those beasts are smurfing!
YUM SCRUNCH CRUNCH YUM GULP SLURP
You know, that gives me an idea! Follow me!
A little later...
I'll need a little more sarsaparilla juice, Smurfette!
Here you go!
Hmm! That sarsaparilla smells good here!
Come closer, Greedy Smurf!
Do you like my sarsaparilla scent, Greedy Smurf?
Aaaah! It's so good! More, more!
PISH PISH PISH
Take those smurfs of sarsaparilla scent and follow me! We have to distance those voracious lizards from the village, for the effect of the kindness perfume won't smurf long!

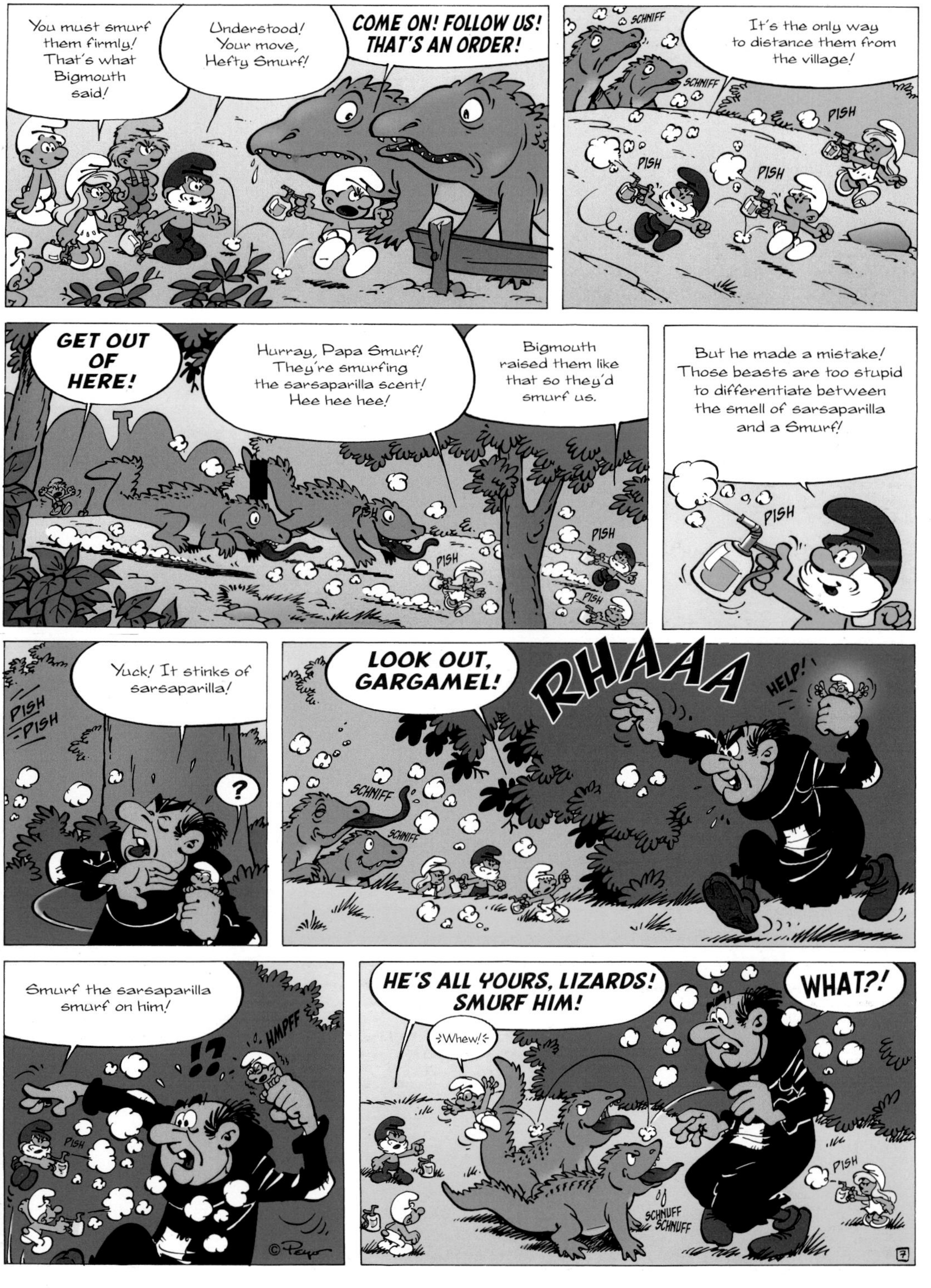
You must smurf them firmly! That's what Bigmouth said!
Understood! Your move, Hefty Smurf!
COME ON! FOLLOW US! THAT'S AN ORDER!
SCHNIFF
SCHNIFF
It's the only way to distance them from the village!
PISH
PISH
PISH
GET OUT OF HERE!
Hurray, Papa Smurf! They're smurfing the sarsaparilla scent! Hee hee hee!
Bigmouth raised them like that so they'd smurf us.
PISH
PISH
PISH
PISH
But he made a mistake! Those beasts are too stupid to differentiate between the smell of sarsaparilla and a Smurf!
PISH
PISH
PISH
Yuck! It stinks of sarsaparilla!
?
LOOK OUT, GARGAMEL!
RHAAA
HELP!
SCHNIFF
SCHNIFF
Smurf the sarsaparilla smurf on him!
!?
HMPFF
PISH
© Peyo
HE'S ALL YOURS, LIZARDS! SMURF HIM!
WHAT?!
Whew!
SCHNUFF
SCHNUFF
PISH
7

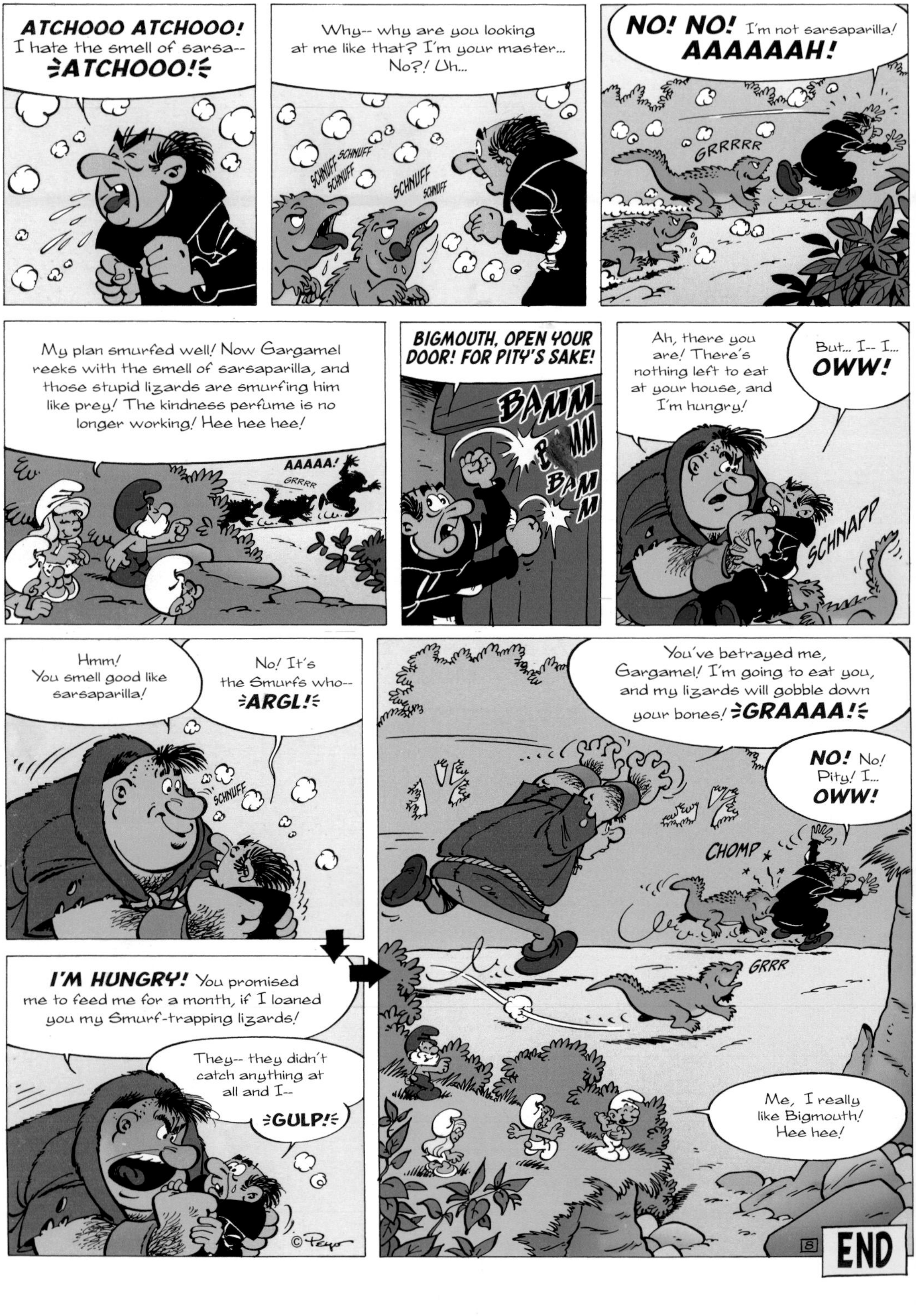
ATCHOOO ATCHOOO! I hate the smell of sarsa-- ATCHOOO!
Why-- why are you looking at me like that? I'm your master... No?! Uh...
SCHNUFF SCHNUFF SCHNUFF
SCHNUFF SCHNUFF
NO! NO! I'm not sarsaparilla! AAAAAAH!
GRRRRR
My plan smurfed well! Now Gargamel reeks with the smell of sarsaparilla, and those stupid lizards are smurfing him like prey! The kindness perfume is no longer working! Hee hee hee!
AAAAA!
GRRRR
BIGMOUTH, OPEN YOUR DOOR! FOR PITY'S SAKE!
BAMM BAMM BAMM BAMM
Ah, there you are! There's nothing left to eat at your house, and I'm hungry!
But... I-- I... OWW!
SCHNAPP
Hmm! You smell good like sarsaparilla!
No! It's the Smurfs who-- ARGL!
SCHNUFF
I'M HUNGRY! You promised me to feed me for a month, if I loaned you my Smurf-trapping lizards!
They-- they didn't catch anything at all and I--
GULP!
© Peyo
You've betrayed me, Gargamel! I'm going to eat you, and my lizards will gobble down your bones! GRAAAA!
NO! No! Pity! I... OWW!
CHOMP
GRRR
Me, I really like Bigmouth! Hee hee!
8
END